The Nanny (T

Vera Roberts

For MES.

This book is a work of fiction. The names, characters, places and incidents are products of the author's imagination, or are used fictitiously. Any resemblance to actual persons, living or dead, events or locales, is entirely coincidental.

Prologue

"Ladies and gentlemen, please buckle up your safety belts as we make our descendent." The captain announced over the PA system.

Tiana Schmidt quickly glanced at her watch and wrapped up her report. The meeting in London had proven to be more successful than she had expected, with the new client happy to sign on with her investment firm. After a short rest at home with her family, she would be refreshed to deliver the strategic planning report in a few days.

When she was younger, she knew was a special kind of weird because she was always fascinated with money—where it came from, how much it could accumulate, and how it was spent. Her love and passion for finance gave boost to her career as an investment banker, eventually leading her to start her own investment firm. She was already a multimillionaire by the time she reached thirty and was projected to be a billionaire by the time she was forty.

Life was good.

As she stared out the window of the plane, Tiana thought about her life. Her friends and family always clamored about how perfect her life was, but Tiana begged to differ. She worked really hard to maintain her professional career, be an attentive mother, and loving wife. While Tiana was a multimillionaire several times over, sometimes she thought she was underpaid. She had to wear many hats, but being a wife and mother were the most important ones. She had sacrificed a lot to her family to make sure they were provided for. But she knew it would be worth it in the end. It always was.

She put away her report and buckled her safety belt. She was anxious to get home. She missed seeing the loves of her life,

Christopher and Tyson, and couldn't wait to see them again. Especially Christopher. Two weeks was way too long to go without sex and she needed to be broken off.

****

"Honey! I'm home!" Tiana called out as she arrived at their mansion.

She dropped off her luggage and hurried upstairs, quickly taking off her clothing. Just thinking about her husband putting his lips on her body made her antsy with anticipation. She masturbated often while she was away; thinking of what her husband was going to do to her. Their sex life had suffered a little upon the birth of their son, but was starting to pick back up again. Christopher was animalistic, devouring her each time with his prowess. He wanted to try new positions and was always ready to go.

Tiana was getting flushed just thinking about it.

She finally reached their bedroom and opened it. "Honey, I've been thinking about this for so…" Her speech stopped short.

Christopher was covering himself and his lady paramour. "Tiana! You're home!" He shifted the young woman off him. She had to have been no more than 18. "I wasn't expecting you home for another few days! Hey, honey!"

Tiana stood in front of her bedroom door and silenced her growing anger. "You get the hell out of my house," she addressed the young woman. "And you?" She turned to her husband. "You follow her."

Christopher hurriedly put on his boxer briefs. "Tee, let me explain…"

Tiana calmly walked over to the bedroom stand and pulled out the loaded 9 mm gun she kept hidden and cocked it. "You have ten seconds," she calmly replied. "One…two…"

Christopher and his lover quickly left the home. In the midst of the drama, Tiana forgot to check to see if Tyson was okay. She rushed over to his nursery and found the three-month old still peacefully sleeping; he completely missed the drama. Tiana softly touched her son's head and loudly sighed. "I guess it's just you and me, baby."

ONE

"You have a business meeting with Michael Lippis at noon; he'll send a car to pick you up. He wants to talk about his portfolio. You have another meeting with the strategic planning team of Kraken Management to discuss their clients. Don't forget your final draft is due to Ebony magazine by the end of the week. Finally, I got you those tickets to tonight's game at Staples Center; the driver will be here around six to pick up you and Erin," Allison Jacobs handed an itinerary to her boss. "Anything else I can do for you, Tiana?"

"Nope, that sounds good," Tiana nodded. "Thanks, Allison."

"Not a problem. Just let me know if you need anything." Allison made her way out of the office.

Tiana looked at her itinerary and briefly wondered how she had time to sleep. Between running her firm, doing a column for a monthly magazine, and making special guest appearances on talk shows, Tiana actually had to pencil in when she needed to sleep at night.

She turned on her computer and was greeted by Tyson's cherub face. How much he had grown over the past few months! He was teething and already out of the clothing she just bought a few weeks ago. Her mother was a doll for watching him, but Tiana knew it was a temporary situation. She never thought she would be a single mother at any point in her life and she needed someone permanent to watch her son as she attended to her career.

"Actually, Allison, could you come back in here for a sec?" Tiana called after her assistant, who promptly came back in. "I need some help with Tyson. As much as I appreciate my mother, a 60-

year-old woman doesn't need to be caring for a six-month-old baby, especially one who's teething. Can you research local nannies and print a list for me?"

"Sure, I'll get right on it," Allison jotted down notes, "when would you need this?"

"Tomorrow, preferably. I need to get someone in soon." Tiana caught a quick glance at a picture of Tyson. "And someone trustworthy."

"Not a problem. I'll have a list by the end of the day." Allison headed out of Tiana's office.

Tiana looked down at the schedule before her and lightly sighed. She had a jam-packed day ahead of her and there wasn't enough time to even breathe. "Okay. Not too bad. A little busy but I'll be okay." Her office phone rang and she recognized the number on the caller ID. "Oh, I don't believe this…" She picked up the phone. "Tiana Morris, speaking."

"The name change that quick, huh?" Her estranged husband, Christopher, spoke over the phone. "I don't remember the divorce being signed off that quickly."

Tiana was always amazed at how her ex could make her go from classy lady to ghetto bitch in just a few seconds but she remained civil. "Christopher, I'm really busy today. What can I do for you?"

"I noticed I no longer have access to our joint account," Christopher replied. "When did you cut off access?"

"I cut off access three months ago," Tiana replied, "you're just now noticing?"

"I need money."

Of course you do. "To spend on your whore?"

"Tiana," Christopher condescendingly began, "let's not make this any uglier than what it is."

"I'm not making it any uglier than what it is," Tiana curtly replied, "you did that without my help."

"I'm contesting the pre-nup." Christopher added.

"Good for you." Tiana dismissed her ex's threat. "Do you plan to see your son anytime within this century?"

"Hire a nanny," Christopher hung up.

Tiana exhaled a sharp breath and put the phone back on the retriever. She opened up her laptop to begin her day. "I should've gotten out of that marriage sooner."

****

"Let's see, what do we have here…Coltrane, Bobby "Blues" Bland, Miles Davis…hmm…" Kieran D'Amato looked at the CDs in his SUV. "I'm going to go with Coltrane today." He popped in the CD and backed out of the parking lot of the extended-stay hotel.

When he was in college, a former girlfriend suggested he listened to jazz as he studied, somehow convincing him the soothing sounds of Ella, Frank, and Louis will make him concentrate better for his exams. She was onto something; Kieran aced his classes and graduated at the top of his class. Throughout the years, Kieran kept up the jazz standards at home and in the office. Especially his office.

The drive to his office was pleasant as always. Hardly any traffic and it was a bright and sunny day in Malibu. He had a busy day already, he could tell. He would have to go to the bank to drop off the deposit. It was payday at the office and he had to ensure everyone received their checks. And then there was that issue about finding a permanent place to stay. He could already hear his mother politely nagging him to move back to Staten Island and help with the family business.

He pulled into the parking lot of Fits and Giggles and turned off the truck. Immediately he was greeted by a screaming child, begging his mother not to leave him. Kieran got out of his truck and walked over to the mother. "First day?" He already knew the answer.

"It is," the mother replied, exasperated. "I'm returning to work and this is not how I wanted to start my first day."

Kieran kneeled down until he was at eye level with the little boy. He pulled out a lollipop and the boy immediately stopped crying. "If you want this, you have to go in there to keep it." Kieran pointed inside.

"Okay!" The boy took the lollipop and left.

The mother was astonished by her son's attitude change. "How did you….?"

"Very few kids turn down candy," Kieran winked before he headed inside.

It was always a maze to get through the place first thing in the morning what with various parents dropping their children off and a few arranging meetings with potential nannies. The staff members were running around trying to get everything settled before it became really chaotic.

It was home sweet home.

"Good Morning, Kieran," Zoe Mitchell greeted her boss. She was a tall female of mixed race, Black and Chinese. She had light mocha skin and a black bob cut that brushed against her jawline. She was lithe like a runway model with the personality of a teenager, an interesting combination that made Kieran not pursue any romantic dealings with her, though he wanted to. Business, never personal, was his motto. He would never date his employees, his clients, or anyone else he had business with. The moment business and personal got mixed up, he would live to regret it.

"Morning, Zoe," Kieran grinned at her as he sat behind his desk. "What's on the agenda for today?"

"Same old, same old. Nothing special. We did have a call come in just now from a potential family," Zoe handed Kieran the information. "High-profile."

Kieran took a quick look at the intake sheet. Tiana Morris. The name sounded vaguely familiar but he couldn't remember the connection. "What's the urgency?"

"Someone soon, preferably today or tomorrow?"

"Today or tomorrow?" Kieran raised an eyebrow. "That's pretty serious."

"I guess. Her assistant said it was serious so I guess time is of the essence."

"Her assistant said it was serious," Kieran repeated with a smirk. He already had a feeling who he was about to deal with. He glanced at the name again. She was probably a singer or an actress. No, she was a stuck-up housewife like he had seen on TV. "I might have to take care of this one, myself. When's the meeting?"

"This afternoon at her home in Pacific Palisades."

"Pacific Palisades, huh?" The Pacific Palisades was a wealthy enclave north of Hollywood and home to many celebrities. Kieran already knew how "serious" the situation was. A woman who probably couldn't stand having her children interrupt her social life. The poor soul probably had to postpone her Botox injections several times already. Kieran looked at his calendar. Other than meeting with his realtor, his day was free. "I need you to drop off the deposit and see that everyone gets paid. I'll make the drive from here to her home. I'll be there for the rest of the afternoon."

"You're going to take on this assignment?" Zoe asked.

"Well, I'm going to check it out at least. I might give it to one of the girls if the lady is legit." Kieran shrugged. "It should be easy. She's probably one of those Housewives on TV and needs the camera time."

"That's a harsh statement about someone you never met," Zoe folded her arms and grinned.

"It's a correct statement about someone I have never met," Kieran added. "A woman living in Pacific Palisades who needs a nanny? It's not rocket science what I'm about to deal with."

Kieran drove to Tiana's home. He parked his SUV by the front gate and looked himself over in the mirror one last time. He popped in a breath mint and slicked back his hair a little. He lightly licked his index fingers to tame down his eyebrows. He wished he'd worn his nice jeans instead. He shook his head. Why did he care about someone he already didn't like?

He got out of the truck and proceeded to walk up the steep driveway to the front door. He had a feeling about the type of family he was interviewing based on the home and the nice Prius parked in the front yard. The man was probably a CEO or doctor. Maybe even a professional athlete. The woman was more than likely a socialite. They might have three kids, including the screaming baby he could hear from the outside.

He looked around the front yard and saw that it was neatly trimmed. *A gardener.* There weren't any toys out in the front. *Strict parents.* To his left, he saw what appeared to be the maid's quarters. *Rich parents.* He rang the doorbell and shoved his hands in his pockets as he rocked back on his heels.

The large front door opened and a Black woman carrying a screaming infant greeted him. "Hello?" Tiana tried to comfort Tyson while giving the same attention to the gentleman before her.

Kieran looked down at a piece of paper. "Tiana Morris?"

"Yes?"

"Hello, I'm Kieran D'Amato." He wanted to shake her hand and not be rude but the woman before him seemed to have trouble of her own. "I'm here for the nanny interview?"

Tiana kept rocking Tyson, hopefully to calm him but the infant seemed to rebuff each movement. "You're Kieran?"

"Yes," The man stated once again.

Tiana had been up all night attending to Tyson and now some attractive man was in her face, applying for a nanny position. She'd missed work due to Tyson being fussy; there was no way she could've gone in looking and feeling the way she was. She was convinced she had not gotten enough sleep and was suffering from illusions. When she saw the name Kieran D'Amato on the list of applicants, she falsely assumed she would be interviewing a woman. "Come in."

Kieran stepped into the palatial estate but didn't look around. He was focused on the child before him. "Allow me, please?" He offered.

"Be my guest," Tiana unloaded her son onto Kieran.

Tyson was screaming so hard, Kieran thought his little lungs were about to burst. "Do you have any hard vegetables in the refrigerator? Like carrots and celery?"

"Sure, follow me." Tiana quickly walked to the kitchen and pulled out a carrot. She gave it to Kieran, who placed it against Tyson's gums. Within a few seconds, Tyson quieted down. "How did you do that?"

"I can tell a teething baby just by the screams," Kieran cooed. "If you had something bursting through your gums, you wouldn't care for it, either."

Tiana smiled for the first time that morning. She had been up all night and was pretty sure she looked as bad as she felt. The man before her was strikingly handsome and she wished she'd put a comb through her hair. She would have, had she known *he* was coming over. "You don't look like a nanny," Tiana noted. Kieran looked more like a Hollywood stuntman than someone who loved to watch kids for a living.

"I'm the owner of Fits and Giggles, the place your assistant called for a nanny. I came here to check out the environment before I sent one of my girls over here." Kieran made eye contact with Tiana and slowly rocked Tyson to sleep. His voice was low and authoritative. "I have a license, child care certification, and several references if you want to check them out. Looks can be deceiving."

Tiana thought back to her wedding day. Everything was perfect. Her Vera Wang gown. Her MAC makeup. Her Jimmy Choos. Her

Neil Lane jewelry. Christopher was dressed in Hugo Boss along with his groomsmen. There were over 400 guests and every table had a miniature wedding cake on it. Christopher promised her forever. That was only three years ago. "Tell me about it," she cleared her throat, "I guess I should formally introduce myself. I'm Tiana Morris and that's my son, Tyson. It's just the two of us here."

Kieran felt like an idiot. He completely miscalculated his estimates by a long shot. No White family of five. No snobby socialite of a wife. No other children. Just a young and wealthy Black single mother. He was confused and impressed at the same time. "Pretty big home for just the two of you."

"I planned to have more," Tiana thought about all the plans she had for her life. Everything was supposed to happen in order: graduate from college, have a career, fall in love, get married, have babies, and live happily ever after. At least five out of six wasn't so bad. "But things happened."

"You don't need to explain. It's none of my business." Kieran gently rocked Tyson.

Tiana grinned. Kieran was surprisingly respectful. She had already made her decision and didn't want to meet with the other applicants. "So when can you start?"

Kieran wasn't planning on being a nanny when he had employees to do that for him. "I'm no longer a private nanny, Ms. Morris—"

"Tiana," she corrected.

"Tiana," Kieran grinned, "so I don't know how I would be of service to you?"

"I don't trust many people, Mr. D'Amato."

"Kieran," he offered.

"Kieran," Tiana replied. "The last nanny I had I found sleeping with my husband. I would prefer a male this time around. You can rest assured that I won't make any advances toward you."

Kieran masked his disappointment. He *wanted* Tiana to make a move. He was so used to the other mothers throwing their tits in his face and wearing the skimpiest of clothing, trying to convince him to give them discounted rates. If they couldn't get the discounted rate, they wanted Kieran to be their side project whenever their husbands weren't home. Kieran knew his appearance was half the reason why so many mothers gave referrals to his business. The other reason was because his child care was the best in Los Angeles.

Still, Kieran sympathized with Tiana. She was a single mother trying to juggle both life and business—a feat incredible for anyone no matter what income level they were. Kieran knew by accepting the gig, he was on the verge of breaking a personal rule. However, he was about to make an exception just for Tiana. He felt an overwhelming need to protect her and Tyson already. "Anytime." Kieran replied as he held a sleeping Tyson.

"What about your business?" She asked.

"I can handle things from a distance. I don't need to be in the office all the time and I have great people who I trust working for me," Kieran rubbed Tyson's back. "I can start today if you want."

For the first time, Tiana took stock of the gentleman before her. He was tall and muscular with dark hair and a five o'clock shadow. He completely filled out his simple attire of a dress shirt and slacks. Kieran was tall, well over six feet, and his presence commanded attention at all times. His eyes were an intense dark that contrasted with his tawny skin. She could smell his cologne and felt her body perspire. There was an electric magnetism between them—sensual, sexual, and intense—and they had barely spoken to each other.

Besides his gorgeous looks, Kieran already showed a warmth and love to Tyson that Tiana hadn't seen from her ex. She had already taken a liking to her new nanny. "I would like that."

****

"I'm taking a private gig, so I won't be around as much," Kieran began as he sat back down behind his desk, "but I'll randomly drop in to make sure you're not running my business into the ground."

Zoe smirked. "You're so mean to me, Kieran."

"You know you love it," he smiled.

"So how did that lady check out?" Zoe folded her arms. "She's legit, I'm assuming? Not a snobby housewife like you thought?"

Tiana checked out just fine. Kieran learned at an early age to check out a woman without being so obvious about it. She was stunningly beautiful with rich, mahogany skin. She had a smile that lit up the room and made her almond eyes sparkle. Her soft brown hair cascaded in long, luscious waves down her back. She had a trim waist, and perky breasts that made Kieran stand to attention. Her simple attire of yoga pants and a tank top hugged her body. She had the beauty to match the brains.

He normally would've given the position to one of his employees and certainly didn't need the money. But he was instantly attracted to Tiana and adored her son already. Even when he left her home, he had an urge to turn around and stay there. Kieran lightly swallowed his feelings. He was breaking a personal rule—the only rule he had—when it came to child care. He would have to be more careful. "She's legit," was all he could reply with.

"Well, let me know if you need anything, Kieran," Zoe left his office.

After Zoe left, Kieran redirected his focus on Tiana. He made a call to one of his friends at the police department and pulled Tiana's private file. He only wished he had done his research on her before he went over to her home. No, it wasn't a home. It was a mansion. Eight bedrooms, nine bathrooms, a basketball court, gym, and Olympic-sized pool and jacuzzi. A three-car garage that housed a Prius.

She drove a Prius. Not a BMW. Not a Mercedes. A Prius.

She earned her fortune through her blood, sweat, and tears. Upon graduating from Howard University magna cum laude with a bachelor's in finance, she completed her MBA at USC. She briefly worked for an investment firm before she left to start her own and amassed her enormous fortune. She was well-respected in the financial sector and was a monthly contributor to a lifestyle magazine, giving out financial tips and advice to other Black women. She was commonly referred to as the Black Suze Orman.

A few years prior, she married hip-hop producer Champagne Cris in what was described as hip-hop meets Wall Street. They were currently involved in an acrimonious divorce, fighting over her fortune. *She has trust issues.* Kieran understood why Tiana was insistent he should be her nanny, and not one of his employees. He had a feeling Tiana probably would've hired whoever he sent to her home if he hadn't made the visit. But he had a policy to check out the residence before he sent his employees over. He wanted to make sure his nannies were going to a place that was safe for them and the children they were caring for.

Kieran tossed the file aside and began making arrangements to spend his next several months—or years—at Tiana's home. He felt uneasy about the assignment already. It was going to be hard to keep his personal feelings separate from his professional side.

TWO

"Your working schedule is from seven a.m. to seven p.m., with weekends off. You will have full access to the house as long as you don't bring any friends over. If they want to visit you, they are more than welcome to see you at the guest house," Tiana walked throughout the house with Kieran, who was holding Tyson. "You get paid twice a month, on the first and fifteenth, and you'll get bonuses pretty much whenever I feel like it."

"Yes, ma'am," Kieran nodded.

"And please," Tiana turned around, "don't call me ma'am. You're older than I am and that's just weird."

Kieran flashed a warm smile. Tiana was only a couple years younger than his thirty-four years. "Okay, Tiana."

Tiana began walking again and led Kieran to his new residence. "If you need supplies, just let me know and I'll give you money for what you need. Don't spend too much because I will research if it's something we really need or you're just being ridiculous."

"That won't be a problem."

"Your rent and board is included in the salary. You're responsible for your own groceries. I have a gardener who comes by once a week for maintenance and the maid comes on Tuesdays." Tiana opened the doors to Kieran's new home. "Welcome home."

Kieran stepped inside the guest house and looked around. It had several bookcases along the wall along with pictures of old Hollywood figures such as Marilyn Monroe, Frank Sinatra, and the Rat Pack. It was already warm and inviting with modern furniture. He walked through the home and it noticed it had two bedrooms and two bathrooms, and it was fully furnished with very nice furniture and electronics. The kitchen was very impressive with all the latest gadgets and probably the biggest refrigerator he had ever seen in person.

The master bedroom had a four post California king-sized bed and candelabras on the walls. It had a romantic feel. All he would have to do was move in, which was fine by him. He didn't have that much to begin with and wasn't missing out on anything in his past. "This is very nice, Tiana."

"Thank you," she politely smiled, "I hope it's too your liking. If there's anything you need, just let me know."

"It's perfect," Kieran's Staten Island baritone boomed throughout the home. "It really is. It's a great place."

"Thank you," Tiana took Tyson away. "I'll leave you to get settled. I'm sure you have a lot of stuff you're moving in."

"I have a few boxes but I should be in by the end of the day." Kieran replied. "I'll let you know if I need anything, though." He warmly smiled.

Kieran's smile was infectious and Tiana smiled back at him. "I hope so."

****

Barbara Berg-Morris had a busy day ahead of her. First, she had a meeting with the scholarship foundation she co-founded. Next, she had afternoon tea with her high-society friends. Finally, she was going to pay a visit to her daughter and possibly talk some sense into her.

Her impending divorce was ruining Barbara's reputation.

For many years, Barbara prided herself on being the example for all women alike. She had the class of Diahann Carroll, the intellect of Phylicia Rashad, and the style of Beverly Johnson. And thanks to her daughter's generous bank account, Barbara was on her way to being wealthy like Oprah Winfrey.

But Tiana's choice in divorcing her husband set Barbara's dreams back. A divorce meant her lifestyle wasn't perfect. Her *life* wasn't perfect. Everyone would be looking at her family and wonder why anyone should listen to them. She couldn't bear to be the joke of her society friends. Not with all she went through trying to learn how to be more presentable.

Dr. Cho, a world-famous plastic surgeon, did her liposuction. Dr. Michaels, the best breast doctor the rich could buy, uplifted her girls. Ms. Joseph, a high-profile hairstylist, added tracks to her hair, creating her luscious and long mane. A personal stylist styled her and kept her wardrobe up to date.

Barbara arrived at her daughter's estate and pulled up in the cul-de-sac driveway. She got out of the car and was greeted by Tiana. "I'm glad to see you drop by, Mother."

"It's been a while since I've seen my daughter and grandson," Barbara gave her daughter a polite kiss and hug before she pulled back. "Tiana, you've gained some weight."

Tiana immediately covered her stomach. She silently admitted she put on a few pounds but it only made her clothes a little snug. She could still fit into them. "Not that much."

"I guess those rose-colored glasses are helping you some," Barbara let herself inside the home.

Tiana rolled her eyes. She loathed seeing her mother, no matter how short the visits were. All her life she was nitpicked at about something frivolous; from the natural style she wore her hair, to why she drove a Prius instead of a BMW, to her clothing choices.

If she didn't have to attend some high-priced gala, she was comfortably dressed as a bohemian love-child, with long, blowy skirts, tank tops, wearing flip-flops, and carrying a hobo bag. She found out she got better treatment when people didn't look at her as if she was a pompous bitch.

Tiana was already dreading her mother's short visit.

She followed her inside her home and promptly started a pot of tea. Barbara always called their mother-daughter visits "tea time" as if it was something pleasant. Maybe it was pleasant for Barbara but it was far from it for Tiana. Tiana knew the "tea time" was Barbara's passive-aggressive way of airing all the grievances she had about her daughter while drinking chamomile tea.

"How are you doing, Mother?" Tiana asked.

"I'm doing just fine. Finally got my life back now that I don't have Tyson keeping my time," she smiled.

"I'm sorry for the inconvenience," Tiana took out a few Oreos and put them on a saucer for her mother. "I've hired a nanny now so you can get back to your meetings and what-not."

"Oh, I didn't mind, but I do think you hiring a nanny was one of your smarter decisions," Barbara glanced down at the Oreos and pushed the saucer away. Just then Kieran entered the kitchen, holding a fussy Tyson. "Well, hello?"

"Hello, ma'am. I'm Kieran." He gently rocked Tyson who was growing fussier by the minute. "I would shake your hand but I'm kinda busy here."

"Oh, let me take my grandson since he's unhappy," Barbara grabbed Tyson from Kieran. "Are you making him a bottle?"

"I was getting ready to do it."

"Well, stop talking to me and get to it," Barbara politely smiled.

Tiana bit her lip to prevent her own sass coming out against her mother. It was one thing to insult her; it was a different ballgame to insult the hired help. "So Mother, what brings this visit?"

"I just wanted to drop in and say hello. I think I'm still allowed to do that, you know." Barbara smiled.

Kieran handed Tyson's bottle to Barbara. "I'll leave you two ladies alone now. Pleasure to meet you, ma'am." He smiled at Barbara.

Barbara looked at Kieran and smiled at him, as he walked away. "He seems like a nice fella."

"Oh, Kieran?" Tiana smiled. They had become great friends over the past few weeks and he brought back something inside Tiana she had lost through her marriage: trust. "He's great, isn't he?"

"He is," Barbara nodded as she fed her grandson. "Have you heard from Christopher lately?"

Tiana felt tension inch up her spine. Just hearing her ex's name made her disgusted. "No, I haven't, Mother."

"You should probably put a call in to him, Tiana. He probably wants to see his son."

"I'm not keeping him from his son, Mother." Tiana knew the truth; each time Christopher called her it was regarding money and not child care. "He can see Tyson whenever he wants."

Barbara wiped Tyson's mouth with his bib. "He made a mistake, Tiana."

"It's not the first mistake, Mother," Tiana argued, "It's the first time I caught him with my own eyes." There were rumors of Christopher's infidelity for a short while and Tiana chose to ignore them even though she knew there was some truth to them. Her philosophy was as long as she didn't see it firsthand and Christopher wasn't so insouciant about his indiscretions, the rumors would stay just that. She should've known better. She was the laughing stock amongst her friends and others all over the world.

No one spoke about Tiana Morris, the woman who founded and ran her own investment company. No one mentioned her articles in many magazines and appearances on daytime talk shows. No, that was boring. Instead, everyone gossiped about Tiana Morris-Schmidt, the woman who was the long-suffering wife of Champagne Cris. They talked about the stories of many side women on gossip boards. They talked about the explicit lyrics Cris rapped about in some songs, lyrics that may or may not have been about her or one of his many side girlfriends. They talked about Cris's girlfriends being so cavalier about their trysts and gifts Cris had given them.

Tiana loosened the tightly clenched fists just thinking about the damage to her reputation caused. Her hard-earned reputation. She would never make that mistake again.

"You should consider counseling," Barbara reasoned. "It worked for me and your father."

Tiana slammed the refrigerator door shut. Did her mother just drop a bombshell on her? "What? Daddy had an affair?"

"Your father had several affairs," Barbara sad matter-of-factly.

Tiana scrunched her nose as she digested the bombshell her mother just gave her. Her father was Prince Charming and a well-respected member of the community. He always adored her mother and showered gifts on her. Tiana often looked at her parents' marriage as ideal. "What?"

"Back in my day, we didn't make such big deal about affairs. You just kept it quiet and moved on." Barbara replied.

Tiana couldn't believe her ears. Everything she knew about her parents' perfect marriage was one big fat lie. "Are you saying I shouldn't have left Christopher?"

"I'm saying Tyson needs both parents in his life," Barbara picked up her grandson and began to burp him. "You should reconsider." She then walked away.

Tiana stood in the middle of the kitchen, exasperated. Her parents always felt they knew what was best for her, without considering her own wishes and needs. "Unbelievable."

"That sounded like an enlightening conversation," Kieran suddenly appeared in the entryway to the kitchen.

"Her and my father always told me what I should've done. If I was too fat, they told me to lose weight. If I didn't get an A on a test, they told me I wasn't trying hard enough. If I wasn't smiling enough, they told me I need to stop with the attitude." Tiana shook her head. "And their whole entire marriage was just a big-ass lie. I was just there to help keep up their façade."

Kieran walked over to Tiana and stood beside her. He put a hand on her back. "You did what you had to do in order to protect you and your son."

Tiana felt the electricity from Kieran's touch. It was warm and comforting. "That doesn't matter to them," Tiana shrugged. "They don't care. I got out of a bad marriage and I ruined their reputation. They always talked about other people's lives and their horrible children but when one of their own makes the gossip rounds, I'm the original sin."

Kieran rubbed Tiana's back, causing small lightning bolts to move up and down her spine. "I still think you rock," he said softly.

Tiana felt a weird tingly sensation. It couldn't have come from Kieran. Did he make a pass at her? No, he didn't. She simply wished he did. It was simply too warm in the kitchen and she needed to open up a window. "Thank you," she quickly moved away to get some fresh air.

"Um, I'm going to take off now unless you need me to stick around?" Kieran offered.

"No, I'll be okay. My mom is here and she likes spending time with Tyson. We'll be fine now."

"Okay," Kieran began to walk away but stopped and turned around. "Say, I'm heading to the farmer's market. Why don't you come with?"

"Farmer's market? What's that?"

"What's that?" Kieran was almost flabbergasted. "Don't you ever venture outside your home and office?"

Tiana was embarrassed at the answer before she even said it. "Not really."

"Come with me," Kieran walked over and pulled Tiana by her arm. "You'll really like it."

"Um, okay," Tiana hurried grabbed her purse and light sweater, "Mom, Kieran and I are going to farmer's market. We'll be right back!" The door closed behind them.

Barbara walked out of the room, still holding Tyson. Her daughter had always made questionable decisions and her choice of nanny didn't go unnoticed by Barbara. Still, she couldn't fault her daughter's behavior. She would've gotten out of her marriage a long time ago if she'd had the same choice.

****

Tiana walked down the street looking around at the various vendors. The aromas of tamales, noodles, smoked meat, and a variety of other ethnic foods tickled her senses, causing them to go into overdrive. She had been used to the bland and beige diet she was on to maintain her figure, she had forgotten what real food smelled and tasted like.

She saw vendors selling beautiful flowers, fruits and vegetables straight from their farms, local bakeries selling their pastries. Children were laughing and playing on a rented bounce house, a street performer was singing an old rock tune, and college students were in a corner haggling over prices of their purchases.

No one was stuffy. No one complained about their gardener or maid. No one complained about the mileage their newest luxury car was getting. Everyone was…real.

"Well, what do you think?" Kieran asked.

"It's so…so…" Tiana inhaled a deep breath and a big smile formed on her face. "…wonderful."

"Isn't it?" Kieran slowly walked down the street, occasionally stopping to check out the local vendors. "I go here all the time to pick up fresh fruit and veggies. Some of the local cuisine is really good as well. Support local farmers and businesses."

"Is it every Thursday?" Tiana asked.

"Yes, from six to nine p.m.," He nodded.

Tiana mentally began penciling in her new schedule. "I guess I can see if I can make some time."

"I think you'll like coming here." Kieran stopped by another vendor and picked up a tomato, examining how ripe it was. "You come once and you'll want to keep coming back."

Tiana watched how gentle Kieran was with the tomato. He slightly squeezed it, trying to feel how soft and firm it was. His hands were big, gentle, and strong and Tiana's thoughts immediately went to how she would like him to apply the same pressure on her breasts as he moved inside her. She quickly snapped out of her thoughts and concentrated on the zucchini before her. "So, do you cook a lot?"

"All the time. I prefer it to junk food." Kieran grabbed a few tomatoes. "I like to eat out occasionally but with restaurants they put so much fat and grease into their food and you never really know what you're eating. When you cook at home, you always know. And besides, what better chef to prepare your meal than yourself?"

"I guess," Tiana had never been much of a cook. It wasn't that she didn't know how to cook; she simply didn't want to. Since her split, she had relied on leftover Chinese food and take-out on the way home. She had gained ten pounds already.

Kieran smiled at Tiana. He found it particularly amusing she was studying the various vegetables in front of her with a scrunched-up nose and pursed lips as if she really didn't know what she was looking at. "Having difficulty deciding?"

"No, it's not that," Tiana rested her chin on a palm. She had eaten out so much within the past week, she was starting to run out of options. "I just don't know what I want for dinner tonight. I hadn't even thought about it."

"I'll make you dinner," he offered.

Tiana looked back up at Kieran and was greeted with another smile, followed by his equally warm eyes. She had never seen such love and compassion in them. "And what's for dinner tonight?"

"Whatever the lady wants," Kieran grabbed Tiana's hand and kissed it, "the lady gets."

****

Tiana looked around at her guest home. She purposely built the guest home so whenever a lot of family and friends came over, they would sleep there and not have to travel to some hotel and spend a small fortune. Truth be told, she'd only had a few people over and it was usually during the major holidays. Now, she was a guest at her own residence.

It was cozy and quaint. Maybe it was little too fabulous for Kieran but he never complained. As she looked around, Tiana saw a little personification from Kieran: his motorcycle helmet on one of the end tables. His vast array of sneakers by the front door. A wide selection of DVDs and blue-ray discs. There were a few pictures of his friends and family.

Tiana got up from one of the bar stools and looked at a framed picture of Kieran and his mother. He towered over her short and stocky frame. She boasted the same huge and welcoming smile he had. "Beautiful woman."

"Yeah, I'm a Mamma's Boy," Kieran glanced over at her as he chopped up vegetables. "It was just me and my brothers growing up. A single woman raising five sons on her own. It wasn't easy."

Tiana thought she had it rough with Tyson. All she had to do was go to work and leave him in the care of someone else for the day.

She had a life of luxury most would dream about and needed to count her blessings. "It doesn't sound like it."

"I'm the second-oldest. My dad left when we were all young; I think my youngest brother, Tony, was no more than a few months old. He just took off one day and that was that. I had a hand in raising all of my brothers."

"Doesn't sound like you had much time for a social life," Tiana commented.

"I was in sports; I played football. I dated a little in high school but it really picked up in college." Kieran quickly sliced the zucchini. "But after everything was done, I was at home doing chores and cooking."

"Cleaning as well?" Tiana rejoined him in front of the bar.

"Oh no," Kieran chuckled, "I don't clean."

"I bet you were real happy with the maid service coming over," Tiana smiled.

"You betcha," Kieran stopped chopping up vegetables and stirred his marinara sauce. "Here, try a taste of this." He scooped a small bit of sauce on a spoon and held it to Tiana's lips.

"Mmm…" Tiana nodded in amazement. "That's delicious! Where did you learn how to cook?"

"Old family recipes," Kieran sprinkled a little more oregano into the sauce. "My mom and *nonna* never wrote down recipes. It was always a little bit of this and a little bit of that. I just happened to pick up some of it."

"Do you speak a little Italian yourself?"

"*Solo un po'*," Kieran smiled, "Just kidding. I'm actually fluent."

"Tell me something in Italian."

"*Il mio nome e'* Kieran. *Sei bellissima. Ti penso sempre e voglio scopare,*" Kieran cooed.

Tiana giggled. "Now what did you just say? For all I know you just told me to clean the kitchen."

Kieran came up with a half-truth. "My name is Kieran. You're beautiful and I think about you all the time," the last part of what he said – *I want to fuck you all night* – he kept silent.

Tiana felt her cheeks turn just a shade of pink. "You're a charmer."

"I can be."

"So tell me about your past?" Tiana leaned on the bar. "What's your history? How did you end up in child care?"

"Grew up in Staten Island, with just my mom, brothers, and grandparents. My real father never bothered. We had plenty of uncles, aunts, and cousins around us. I joined the Army when I was fresh out of high school and did a couple of tours. I wanted to see the world and get some money for college. When I got home, I went through some personal drama but once I got back on my feet, I enrolled in college to study early childhood education and started my business a few years ago. Being a nanny can be lucrative but you really have to love kids and well, I really love kids." Kieran began slicing bread. "Haven't looked back since. I'm in the middle of trying to find a permanent place so I was staying at an extended-stay hotel. I'll start looking again once this assignment ends." He flashed a welcoming smile.

Tiana felt her heart collapse. Kieran had only been there for a short time yet she wanted him to stay forever. "That's simple and straight to the point. Sounds a lot better than my boring story."

"Boring?" Kieran questioned. "You live in a mansion and you're a millionaire. What's so boring about that?"

"I worked really hard to get to where I am. I'm not a trust fund baby or got rich because of some dude," Tiana defiantly said, "I really wanted to know more about money and all that entails. It's just my personal life, I wasn't smart about that."

Kieran thought back to his own past; he knew all too well what Tiana was talking about. "Tell me about it if you want."

"I think I got married, not because I was in love but, because I thought Christopher was safe." Tiana admitted.

Kieran was intrigued. "What do you mean?"

"I was impressed by him. He was a hip-hop producer; he had his own label. When I first went into his office, I saw all these diamond and gold records. I thought I found someone who wasn't trying to rob me of my fortune." Tiana reminisced. Christopher would take her on shopping sprees and they would walk the red carpet at industry events. "He bragged about me to his friends and family; mentioned me in interviews. It was perfect."

"So what happened?"

Tiana stared out into a blank space and her mood quickly turned somber. "It wasn't perfect. I wasn't the only one; I was just number one. There was a number two, three…seven, eight, nine…who really knows? I found out the money we had in our joint account been being spent on his Ho of the Week. I stopped funding it due to my suspicions. And do you know what he had the nerve to ask me? That fool had the nerve to ask if everything was okay at work and if I was going broke!"

Kieran poured Tiana a glass of wine and slid it to her. He knew heartbreak all too well. When he returned home from serving overseas, all he found was a Dear John letter from his ex and his clothing. He was fortunate that he had family who provided him with hot meals and a roof over his head until he got back on his feet.

"I was stupid enough to think that if we had a baby, it would stop. So we got pregnant and all it did was just increase his appetite. I came home one day from a business trip and well, that was it." Tiana took a big gulp of the sweet wine. "Anyway, enough of my pathetic sob story. I'm sorry I ruined dinner."

"No, not at all," Kieran grabbed Tiana's hand and gave it a gentle squeeze, "not at all. Thank you for being comfortable enough to share it with me."

Kieran's touch shot through Tiana's body like a gun. It was electric. It was magnetic. It was something she hadn't felt before. "You will make a woman so lucky one day," Tiana smiled, "you will be a great boyfriend to somebody."

Kieran slightly hoped Tiana was referring to herself. There he went again with his personal feelings getting in the way of his professionalism. "You think so?"

"I know so." Tiana smiled, "You're hot, you're smart, and you're great with kids. Tyson just adores you! What woman wouldn't find that attractive?"

"Thank you for the compliment," Kieran began to fix plates, "but I'm not interested in dating anyone."

"Why not?"

Because the woman I really want is in front of me. Kieran erased the thought from his head. "I'd rather devote all my time and energy in watching Tyson."

"That's a sweet gesture, but you need a life besides me and my son," Tiana suggested, "You need a woman."

Kieran couldn't have disagreed more. All he wanted was to watch over Tiana and Tyson. His heart opened for both of them to reside permanently in there. "So you say."

After the delicious dinner, Kieran walked Tiana back to the front door of her home. "You didn't have to walk me here. I know my own house."

"I'm not letting a lady walk home when it's already dark," Kieran insisted. "I don't care if it's in your compound or if you live next door."

Tiana smiled warmly. She never had a man go out of his way show her…what was that thing she never got from her ex…oh yes, respect. It was something she could quickly get used to. "Thank you, Kieran."

"You're welcome, Tiana." They arrived at her front door. Both had awkward stances about how to proceed next. "I'll guess I'll see you tomorrow morning?" Kieran finally broke the ice.

"I guess so," Tiana wanted Kieran to make a move on her but hid her true feelings. She also didn't want to compromise their working relationship. "I'll see you tomorrow morning, Kieran."

"Bye, Tiana. Sweet dreams." He winked and walked off.

Tiana watched him walk into the darkness and listened for the door to his home to close. She then leaned against her front door and sighed. Kieran went against every stereotype she ever thought of and was straight out of the fantasy pages of a romance novel. He would make one woman very lucky one day. "Sweet dreams, Kieran."

THREE

"TeeTee!" Erin Kressley greeted her best friend. She was a full-figured Black female who grew up with Tiana. She often wore wigs to change up her hairstyle to go along with her eclectic personality. When Tiana went into the financial sector, Erin went into the performance arts and became a back-up singer for several A-list stars. They had known each other since middle school. "Girl, you blow up and become Ms. Fancy Executive and we never see you anymore!"

Tiana bounced Tyson on her hip. "I'm trying to get my groove back like Stella, if you forgot."

"How is everything?" Erin asked. "How's Chris? Has he been in contact?"

"When he wants money," Tiana shook her head, "I'm starting to believe that's why he wanted me to begin with."

"Unbelievable," Erin commented.

"No, actually it is pretty believable," Tiana replied.

"What's unbelievable is the piece of eye candy walking towards us," Rocio Martinez eyed Kieran. Rocio was Tiana's other best friend. She was a tall, model-esque Latina with silver eyes and a long, black mane. She was happily married to an NBA player and expecting their first child. "Who is that?"

"Who's what?" Tiana asked.

"That fine specimen walking over to us," Erin took notice.

Tiana turned around and waved at Kieran. "Oh, that's Kieran. He's my new child care provider."

"Child care provider?" Erin asked. "Is that a fancy way of saying *nanny*?"

"Nanny?" Rocio eyed Kieran as he approached the women. "Is that what they're calling the escort services nowadays?"

"Stop it," Tiana greeted Kieran with a hug. "Kieran, these are my friends, Rocio and Erin. Girls, this is my nanny…"

"Yeah, yeah, whatever…" Erin sashayed her way to the man with olive skin and ebony hair. "Hi, I'm Erin but you can call me whatever you want."

"Pleasure to meet you, Erin," Kieran flashed a warm smile towards the young beauty.

"It can be," Erin winked.

"Girl, stop," Tiana shook her head. "You're a few months away from getting married."

"Yeah, but there's nothing wrong with looking, huh?" Erin looked around Kieran's hands and noticed there wasn't a wedding band. "How are you doing, handsome?"

"I'm doing just fine, Erin." Kieran shoved his hands in his jeans pockets. "How are you this wonderful day?"

"It's much better now," Erin flirted.

"Okay," Tiana stood in between Kieran and her friends. "Enough introductions here. Kieran needs to rest. He just moved in recently."

"It's fine, Tiana," Kieran smiled. "It's nothing."

"So handsome," Erin moved her way towards Kieran, "how do you like working for Tiana? I know she's a pain in the ass."

"Erin!" Tiana was embarrassed for her friend.

"It's cool," Kieran smiled. "I don't mind being in the company of beautiful women."

"Oh, he's definitely a keeper," Rocio nudged Tiana with an elbow, who shushed her friend. "So TeeTee, are you ready for the BBQ?"

"Yeah, I just need to go grab Tyson's diaper bag and stroller then we can go," Tiana replied.

"Hey, Kieran, what are you doing today? Why don't you come with us?" Rocio asked. "You can get some great food and there's plenty of adult interaction."

"Well, if it's okay with Tiana," he suggested, "I don't want to intrude on her private life."

"What private life?" Erin smirked. "I'm sure she has cobwebs in places cobwebs shouldn't be."

"Erin!" Tiana didn't know if she was more embarrassed for her or her friend. She turned to her nanny. "Kieran, if you want to come with us, that's perfectly fine by me. You don't need my permission to do anything."

"I would love to come," he warmly smiled, "let me go grab my jacket and I'll meet you ladies back here." He then walked off.

Rocio and Erin admired the sight of Kieran's tight ass as he left. "So how is he in bed?" Rocio asked.

Tiana looked at her friend in shock. "You know I would've expected that comment from *that one* but not from you," she referred to Erin.

"Oh, come on, TeeTee! He's freaking gorgeous and he's *just* your nanny? Girl, bye!" Rocio shook her head. "He likes you, you know that?"

"He likes me as his employer," Tiana added. "We have a strictly professional relationship. We've only hung out a little since he started a short while ago."

"Well, this couldn't have been any better!" Erin smiled. She loved playing matchmaker to her friends. "I say this is a great opportunity for the two of you to get to know each other and maybe you won't be so stuffy."

"I'm not stuffy," Tiana defended. "I'm just not ghetto fabulous."

Rocio and Erin looked at each other. "Stuffy." They said in unison.

****

"Well, well, well...look who decided to come by and entertain us little folk," Tiana's longtime friend, Timothy, greeted her with a big hug. He was a Black man of average build with a light goatee and nice fade. "You blow up and act like you can't be around us anymore."

"Okay, whatever, big-shot music video director," Tiana laughed. "Whatever."

"Don't hate the player, hate the game," Tim turned to Kieran, "what's up, man? I'm Timothy but you can call me Tim."

"Hi, Tim. I'm Kieran and I'm Tiana's..."

"...friend!" Tiana blurted. "He's my friend. I just brought him along with us."

"Nice to meet you, Tiana's *friend*," Tim rolled his eyes. "Anyway, man, do you want a drink? Let me hook you up with a soda. Follow me." Tim and Kieran left.

Rocio and Erin appeared from behind Tiana. "Yeah, that wasn't obvious," Rocio mentioned.

"I am not going to have Kieran introduce himself as my *nanny* here in front of everyone," Tiana stated. While she had no problem with Kieran being her nanny, she was still getting used to the fact she had to refer him as such. "That is embarrassing."

"For you or him?" Erin asked.

"I am trying to protect him," Tiana dropped her shoulders. "I know how a man's pride can be."

"Kieran didn't mind being called your nanny, TeeTee," Rocio commented. "You're the one with the issue with it."

"And what is that supposed to mean?" Tiana folded her arms.

"Should I tell her?" Erin asked Rocio.

"Yeah, I think you should tell her..." Rocio replied back.

Tiana folded her arms. "Tell me what?"

"Please remove that giant stick from up your ass," Erin suggested. She turned to Rocio. "Was that good?"

"Yeah, that was good," Rocio nodded. "Straight to the point, I think."

"I do not have a giant stick up my ass! I am just...just...protective of my brand." Tiana defended as they walked over to the bar.

"TeeTee—I'm still allowed to call you that, right?" Rocio asked as Tiana shot her a death look. "You're among friends, people you have known since middle school. Let it go and have some fun today. Let loose." Rocio handed Tiana a drink. "Drink up."

"I'm not drinking with my son around," Tiana said.

"Kieran is here to watch Tyson and he's not drinking. Have one. Have two." Erin poured a half-glass of lemonade and topped it with Grey Goose. "Please, for my sake. You're killing my buzz and I'm not even drunk yet."

****

"So how did you and Tiana know each other?" Tim asked.

"I'm her nanny," Kieran replied as he managed to fix a plate of food while holding Tyson.

"Her nanny, huh?" Another man, Jeremy, chimed in. He was an Hispanic male who looked like he could be a model instead of a movie producer, with his chiseled body and structured jawline. He was happily married to his high school sweetheart. "I wish I got paid to watch my kids. I would enjoy it more."

"How many do you have?" Kieran asked.

"Two and that's plenty." Jeremy added. "Two-year-old twins."

"Ouch," Kieran added.

"Exactly. Ouch." Jeremy nodded. "I have an empty wallet and I get no sleep. But I wouldn't trade it for the world, though."

"I hear that," Kieran followed the men to a picnic table. "So you all have known each other since middle school?"

"Yep. We all grew up together in Baldwin Park. We were all involved in the arts or what-not and just stuck together." Another man, Matthew, joined in. He was a Black male with an athletic build and bald head. He was a pediatrician and engaged. "We were called the Us-8 in high school because well, it's always been *us eight*. Me, Tim, Jeremy, Chad, Tiana, Rocio, Erin, and Denise. No matter what we all do, we always get together every couple of months for a BBQ to kinda check in on one another."

"That's cool you all kept in touch throughout the years," Kieran held Tyson on his lap while he began to eat lunch.

"We can't get rid of each other, though we tried with some," Matthew added as he spotted Chad and Denise walking together. "Like those two."

Kieran looked up and saw a Black man dressed in the flashiest clothes he had ever seen and a light-skinned Black female in short-shorts and an equally short tank top and high heels. "Who are they?"

"The broke-ass Brad and Angie," Tim commented.

"This generation's Ike and Tina," Jeremy commented.

"Wouldn't that be Chris Brown and Rhianna?" Matthew asked.

"Oh yeah, it would be," Jeremy agreed.

"Fellas," Chad approached the picnic table with Denise on his arm. "I see you have started without me, as usual."

"The picnic started two hours ago, Negro," Tim commented.

"The party starts when I arrive," Chad flashed a smile.

"There are no cameras here, man," Tim replied. "You can cut that out now."

"Hi, there," Chad made his way over to Kieran and sized him up. "I'm Chad. You may know me as the greatest running back of all time."

"The greatest over-hyped and *former* running back of all time," Tim chimed in.

"That's until I get a deal with a team. It's still early so anything can happen," Chad licked his lips and smiled. "That's all."

"Day-dreaming ain't just for kids," Matthew commented.

****

"So TeeTee, who's the man holding Tyson?" Denise asked as she fixed a plate.

"That's Kieran. He's my…" Tiana felt Erin's and Rocio's eyes on her. "…he's my nanny."

"Your nanny, huh?" Denise looked back at Kieran. "Is he single?"

"He is, but you're not," Rocio added.

"Thank you," Erin nodded.

"What? Me and Chad are just friends," Denise examined a piece of chicken before putting it on her plate.

"Oh, so y'all broke up again?" Erin asked. "This would be the fifty-eleventh time, right?"

"If you two broke up, why did you come here with him?" Tiana asked.

Denise scoffed. "My Benz is in the shop and I wasn't about to take the bus," she tossed her blond mane behind her. "Besides, he owed me a favor and offered to take me."

"Do you want to know?" Erin asked Rocio.

"No, but she's about to tell us, anyway," Rocio rolled her eyes.

"I pulled some strings to get him an audition," Denise smiled like she made a major announcement.

"Did those pulled strings require knee pads?" Erin asked.

"And some toothpaste for afterwards?" Rocio smiled.

"Anyway," Denise dismissed their comments, "we're still friends and occasionally have sex but we're free to see other people."

"I'm glad you two are friendly," Tiana sipped her lemonade.

"Yeah, me too," Denise sat next to her, "so tell me more about Kieran…"

****

"So, you're Tiana's nanny, eh?" Chad bit into his ribs and eyed Kieran. He didn't know too much about the man but already knew he didn't like him. Anyone he didn't know, Chad already didn't like. "How much do you make?"

Kieran studied Chad's demeanor. He knew who he was the moment Chad approached him. Chad Thomas. The darling running back of University of Texas. Heisman trophy winner. Number one NFL draft pick. Spent fourteen long years in the NFL, eventually winning two Super Bowl championships. Was as notoriously known for his womanizing, wild parties, and illegitimate children as he was for his performance on the field. He still had hopes of being back on the field, despite just scoring a lucrative gig as an analyst.

Furthermore, Chad was particularly interested in Tiana—either her body or her money, Kieran couldn't quite decide which one came first. "Quite a bit," Kieran bounced Tyson on his lap.

Chad chewed his ribs and continued to eyeball Kieran. "How much is that?"

"I don't discuss money matters," Kieran replied.

"Well, I do," Chad let out a loud burp, causing the other men to look at him with disgust. "I know who much every *nigga* at this table makes but you."

"Negro, you don't know how much I make," Tim shook his head.

"Same here," Jeremy agreed.

"Sign me up on that list," Matthew added.

"Well, I know the ballpark," Chad took a swig of his beer. "And I want to know who's the guy around my money!" His admission caused an amusing smile from Kieran. "I mean, Tiana's money."

Kieran's eyes narrowed on Chad. He knew his type without getting to know the man. He was all talk and little substance. He also had a feeling Chad's interest in Tiana wasn't that of a kind friend, but a dejected love interest looking for a come-up. "Out of curiosity, does Tiana know about your interest in her?"

"No," Chad took a swig of his beer.

"I will make sure she knows," Kieran smiled. "Excuse me, gentlemen. I need to change someone's diaper." He got up and left.

"Make sure you wipe Chad's ass nice and clean," Matthew chimed in to laughter around him.

"That's not funny, brah," Chad glared at his friend.

"No, you begging for Tiana's money kinda is," Tim added.

****

Denise watched Kieran go inside the home and saw an opportunity. "Excuse me, ladies. I'll be right back." She went inside the home.

"*Please* take your time," Erin commented. She waited until Denise was out of earshot. "She has her eyes set on Kieran, TeeTee. Watch out for that one."

"She has her eyes set on every man she meets," Tiana rolled her eyes. "Kieran is no different."

"And what if he likes her back?" Rocio asked.

"And Kieran brings her over while you're at work?" Erin prodded.

Tiana swallowed the lump in her throat. She thought she felt something for Kieran the other day but was convinced it was just the weather change. "Well, I told Kieran he could only have visitors at the guest house."

"And what if Tyson is not being properly cared for because Kieran is mesmerized with fake titties in his face all day long?"

"*All* day long," Rocio added.

Tiana felt a swell of jealousy. Her breathing became constricted. "Fuh…fuh…forget it!"

"Damn!" Erin snapped her fingers. "Almost got her to say *fuck*!"

"Next time, though," Rocio patted Erin's shoulder. "Next time."

"Besides, Kieran would never blatant disrespect me like that! He would never do anything so rude, so vile, so…" Tiana's eyes widened as she caught a glimpse of the sight before her.

Erin and Rocio looked over to see what stopped Tiana's soliloquy. They both smiled at the impending drama. "Oh, it's about to be on!" Rocio smiled.

Kieran and Denise walked out of the home together. Denise was holding Tyson while Kieran carried the diaper bag. Denise gave Tyson to Chad while Kieran set down the diaper bag. She then grabbed Kieran's hand and walked him over to an empty spot by the DJ booth and began dancing.

As they seductively danced, Kieran placed a firm hand on the small of Denise's back as their legs intertwined and their bodies ground against each other. Denise's hands held onto Kieran's muscular arms and her eyes were closed. She was mouthing something, Tiana figured. It was something wrong. It was something naughty.

Denise was mouthing, *fuck me, Kieran.*

Tiana's eyes widened. She gulped some more of her vodka lemonade. Jealousy sliced through her body like a knife. "Who does that hussy think she is? Flirting with *my* nanny? And holding *my* baby? I'll show her!" Tiana took another swig of lemonade.

Erin poured some more vodka in Tiana's glass. "Do it, girl!"

Rocio removed Tiana's hoop earrings. "Kick her ass, girl!"

Tiana finished the last of her drink. "I'm going to!" She marched over to Kieran.

Rocio and Erin watched the impending drama from the sidelines. "You think she's going to do it?" Rocio asked.

Erin shook her head. "Not a chance."

****

"Excuse me!" Tiana said in a tone that was just short of yelling. "Can I interrupt this dance?"

Just when Denise was about to tell Tiana where to go with the horse she rode on, Kieran interrupted her. "Sure, Tiana. Excuse me, Denise," Kieran offered a hand to Tiana, who took it and gave a smarmy smile to Denise.

The hypnotic beat of Patra's "Worker Man" blared through the speakers. Tiana swayed her hips to the beat, closing her eyes and caressing her skin as she felt the rhythm take over her mind. She felt Kieran's hands on hips and they moved together in unison, dancing together as one. She felt his breath on her neck and pushed more into him, wanting to get closer and closer to him.

Tiana turned around and locked eyes with Kieran. It was as if they were the only ones at the BBQ. All she heard was the music and the pounding of her heartbeat. All she smelled was his cologne with notes of musk, earth, and wood, intoxicating her nose. All she felt were his eyes drinking her in, his sporadic breath fighting to keep steady, and his strong hands wrapped around her body, daring to go lower but holding steady at the small of her back.

I want you, Tiana. I want you. Tiana hoped Kieran's eyes were sending the signs she desperately wanted read.

It's yours for the taking, Tiana's eyes spoke back to him.

They inched closer to each other's face, their lips touching but not kissing. They were so close, so close and…

"Oops, my bad!" Chad waved. "Sorry about that."

Tiana and Kieran glared at the man. He somehow bumped into the DJ booth and scratched the record, sending them both crashing back down to a harsh reality.

FOUR

The hustle and bustle of the morning hours never got old.

After settling into a routine, Kieran knew Tiana's schedule like the back of his hand. Sometimes she'd be home after seven, but never later than eight. They made weekly outings to the farmer's market and he would cook dinner for her the same night as they reminisced over past loves, youthful mistakes, and current topics.

Every morning was always the busiest. Kieran would wake up and shower quickly. About thirty minutes later, he arrived at Tiana's front door and opened it with the key she had given him. He always made a bee-line straight to Tyson's nursery and made the little boy his breakfast of pureed pears and formula.

Then he just waited.

He listened intently as Tiana rushed back and forth between her walk-in closet and her bedroom, all the while muttering to herself about something. Sometimes she talked about a presentation. Sometimes she complained about one of her colleagues or competitors. Mostly, the utterances were about her looks. She couldn't find the right blush. She couldn't find the right pair of shoes. She swore she'd ironed a particular pair of pants.

Kieran found it amusing.

It reminded him of when he dated and how he would wait for what felt like hours for the woman to get ready. When she was finally ready, all Kieran would think about was how soon she was able to get out of the same outfit she spent so long trying to get into.

He loved Tiana's professional look. She would wear the sharpest business suits and heels with bright, beautiful colors such as orange, yellow and red to contrast with her milk chocolate skin tone. She never wore her long locks down and always had her hair up in a bun. She was the epitome of looking like a million bucks.

Her makeup was nude and only enhanced her beautiful almond-shaped eyes and full lips. And the walk she had; she walked around as if she ruled everything. Kieran never thought he could be so enamored with a take-charge woman.

Enamored?

He could admit he was attracted to Tiana the moment he saw her. She was graceful, elegant, intelligent, and beautiful. She had an aura about her and her sensuality smoldered underneath her designer garb. He often fantasized about her during many masturbation sessions when he was alone in his home, wondering how hot her mouth would be on his cock and the swell of her breasts as they bounced when she would ride him. He wanted her to wrap her legs around his waist as he moved inside her, taunting her with his words, hands and mouth as he pushed in and out of her heat.

She was also out of his league. A multi-millionaire woman doesn't fall in love with a guy from Staten Island. Her ex-husband was a hip-hop producer and several of her other exes were wealthy and prominent like she was. He had seen her wardrobe, which boasted of many designer names—half he couldn't pronounce. Her home was probably worth more than what he would make in his lifetime.

And when they seductively danced against each other…he felt how soft and lithe her body was. The way she ground against him, as if her body was begging and *daring* him to touch her, taste her, and please her. All Kieran wanted to do was pick Tiana up and take her inside Tim's house, spending the rest of the afternoon making love to her.

It was a nice fantasy. After the dance, they avoided each other for the rest of the BBQ until it was time to leave. When they arrived home, Tiana had sobered up and acted like the dance never took place. She returned to her professional demeanor and that was that.

He hated how he fell in love. He fell hard and fast, almost to the point of ridiculous. After a failed marriage, Kieran made it a point to not get too involved with any woman and kept a rotating door of dates throughout the years. He didn't mind bringing up the subject of marriage and children but when the woman brought it up, Kieran quickly lost interest. He felt suffocated and had to leave.

He made the mistake of living with his last girlfriend at her home. When the relationship ended, Kieran found himself out of a permanent residence. The nanny position was a good thing for him. He could live in his own quarters and not worry about anything else.

Still, the thoughts of wanting to be with Tiana weren't making it easier. The kicker was that Tiana insisted Kieran go out and find a date. She was persistent in telling him that; despite Kieran hinting he wasn't interested in dating.

"Okay, I should be home sooner than seven tonight, but I'll call once I know for sure," Tiana yelled out as she walked downstairs, "and then you're free to do whatever."

"Good," Kieran wiped Tyson's mouth. "I have a date tonight at eight so I'll need the extra time to get ready for it."

Tiana stopped shuffling and felt a strange sensation. Her lips turned downward and a tight squeeze set upon her heart. Was that her fists clenching tight? Why did she suddenly feel the need to hand out a beat down? "A date, huh?"

"Yeah, I finally took your advice and got me a date," Kieran looked up at Tiana, "I'll let you know how it goes."

"Yeah," Tiana swallowed her pride, "please do."

****

"Is everything okay, Ms. Morris?" Allison knocked on her door.

Tiana shook her head. How long had she been staring into space? How long had Allison been there watching her? Why was she so preoccupied with Kieran and his date? All day she had been wondering if he was still going to go out with that chick. She didn't even know the girl's name but she already labeled her as *that chick.* She was probably stuck-up and fluffy and had no ass.

What the hell? Where was that attitude coming from? Tiana was amazed with herself—how mean and catty she had become. She never cared this much about her ex-husband; and here, all of a sudden, Kieran was bringing out the worst in her. Ooh, he was oh-so bad for her in an oh-so good way. "Yeah, I'm fine. I have a lot on my mind. What's up?"

"Oh, nothing. I just wanted to see if there was anything you wanted me to do before I leave tonight?" Allison asked.

Tiana looked down at her watch. It was almost 5:30 and by the time she got home, she would be seeing Kieran get ready to leave for his date. There was that uncomfortable feeling forming in the pit of her gut, now accompanied by her rapidly beating heart. What was that? "No, I'm fine. Thank you, Allison. Have a good night."

****

"And there's mommy!" Kieran handed a giggly Tyson over to Tiana and gave her a light hug. "How was your day?"

"It was…" Tiana barely got any work done and she had Kieran to blame. "It was…productive. How was your day with this one here?"

"It was good. We played, napped, and had fun between us bros. Ain't that right, little man?" Kieran tickled Tyson, who simply smiled back at him.

Tiana's heart warmed upon seeing the interaction between Kieran and her son. She wanted that forever. *Wait, what? What is going on with my feelings?* "Good! I'm glad you had fun."

"Well, I should be going now," Kieran grinned, "I'll let you know how it goes tomorrow morning."

"Okay," Tiana secretly wanted him to have a bad date. "Have fun!" *Please don't.*

Kieran smiled at Tiana. He wished he was going out on a date with her instead of some floozy he met online. "I'll try."

****

Kieran sprayed some cologne on himself before doing a quick glance over in the mirror one last time. He chose a simple attire of a shirt and jeans. It was dinner and a movie-type of date with a woman he met online. It wasn't a date he was particularly looking forward to. The woman was nice enough and very attractive but that was it.

She didn't have the same passion and intensity Tiana had. She didn't have that fire. She didn't have the aura, the sensuality, the warmth, the intellect of his employer.

Get a grip, bro, Kieran said to himself. He could be attracted to Tiana all he wanted but he knew his role in her life. He was her child's nanny; an employee. Tiana was not going to date the help.

He could only hope and fantasize that she would make an exception.

Kieran grabbed his keys and headed out. Maybe he'd get a little lucky tonight. It would certainly take his mind off Tiana.

****

Tiana sat at the kitchen counter nursing her Merlot and going over a financial report. She had given Tyson a bath and put him to sleep a short while before and was enjoying her quiet time. It was just her thoughts and work keeping her company.

Tiana glanced over the financial report one last time and put it away. It was time for her to have some nonsensical fun. She was going to purchase something expensive and frivolous just because. She was in the mood to spend a ton of money and she had a disposable bank account.

Plus, it would take her mind off Kieran for the time being.

She wondered how Kieran's date was going. He had been gone for two hours and she couldn't help but steal glances at the clock every so often. She imagined he probably took his date out dancing, maybe they took in a flick. Maybe they went for a stroll along the beach.

She quietly imagined it was her on a date with Kieran.

"Are you enjoying your evening, *bella*?" Kieran asked as he fed Tiana a chocolate-dipped strawberry.

"Mmm, very much, baby." The fire softly crackled as the pair lay on the bearskin rug.

"I can't wait until later," Kieran opened his mouth and let Tiana feed him a strawberry.

"What's for later?" Tiana smiled. Kieran nodded towards the bedroom and winked at her. "Well, if that's the case, why wait?" She grabbed Kieran's hand and led him to her bedroom.

He pressed his body against hers and reveled in her softness. His hands caressed her back and he forcefully pushed her face away, exposing her neck. He caressed the hollow of it with an index finger, eliciting a soft moan and shivers from Tiana. "Kieran…" she breathed.

"Shh…" His crushed his lips against her neck and Tiana moaned in pleasure. Kieran softly kissed along her jawline, eventually meeting her lips with his. His tongue waltzed with hers and she had never felt such a yearning inside her body before. She loved the soft roughness of his tongue and how experienced his lips were as they kissed all over her body.

"Damn, Tiana," Kieran moved her hand to his cock, "you feel that, *bella*? You feel what you did to me?"

"I want you inside me," Tiana whispered.

Their clothing disappeared and the next thing Tiana knew, she and Kieran were sitting naked in bed, facing each other. He was guiding her as she rode his cock, her arms tightly wrapped around his neck. He captured one breast in his mouth and flipped Tiana on her back, thrusting hard inside her, his balls caressing her pussy with each stroke. Their lips captured each other's as their bodies steadily climbed to their orgasms.

The mood was so perfect; if only Tyson would stop crying…

The sound of her son being fussy brought Tiana out of her fantasies. She knew it was too good to be true.

****

Kieran arrived home from his interesting date. Although his date was entertaining enough, he didn't foresee them dating in the near future. He should've known better than to hit on a chick who was barely eighteen and acted like it.

He noticed Tiana's living room light was still on and he took a chance on seeing if she was still up. He entered the key in the door and quietly opened it. He found Tiana quietly sitting on the sofa with her reading glasses on and perusing her laptop.

"You're still up?" Kieran smiled as he entered the front door.

"Looking at overpriced handbags," Tiana took off her glasses and smiled back. She had grown to love seeing his face every day. "How was your date?"

Kieran shook his head and took a spot next to Tiana on the couch. "The last time I will date anyone younger than I am, ever again."

"Ouch," Tiana nursed her sweet wine. "That bad, huh?"

"Great girl, but she's eighteen. Other than a good time in bed, I really don't know what I'll be able to do with her."

"I'm sure you can do some things with her."

Kieran cocked his head to the side. "Name one."

Tiana thought quickly. "You can take her to the eighteen and over clubs."

"Oh yes, so I can spend more time at Romper Room," Kieran chuckled.

"At least you found out early enough," Tiana pointed out.

"Saves me a lot of heartache and B.S. down the line, that's for sure," Kieran sighed. "Tyson asleep?"

"Soundly and peacefully." Tiana smiled. "Thank God."

"You like your quiet moments, I take it."

"I love my son. Absolutely in love with him." Tiana took another sip of wine and finished her glass. "But when it's quiet, it's soooooo nice!" She chuckled.

"I bet it is," Kieran smiled.

Tiana took off her glasses and closed her laptop. "I want to thank you for being here. You don't know how much it means to me to have someone in the house to take care of my son while I'm away at work. I don't have to worry if he's okay or getting adequate care. I just focus and concentrate on my job." She reached over and grabbed Kieran's hand. "So, I thank you for doing that."

"Tiana, it's my job to make sure you don't worry about home when you're away," he slightly rubbed her hand. It felt like satin. "I wouldn't be doing my job if you were checking in all the time."

"Thank you, Kieran." Tiana moved closer to him and climbed on top of him. "It means a lot to me."

Kieran felt Tiana's heat through her skin. Her breasts pressed against his chest and he felt his mouth water just thinking about how wonderful they would feel in his mouth. Her sensuality screamed aloud and he knew if he made just one movement, Tiana would be naked and writhing underneath him as he pleasured her, licking her heat, playing with her pearl and her nipples, and caressing her toned legs as they pressed against his chest.

Kieran also knew Tiana was drunk off her rocker. She may have been calmly sipping from her wine glass when he stopped by, but he could tell by the empty bottle on the table, it wasn't her only glass that night. "Tiana, you're drunk," Kieran stated as a fact.

"Mmm…maybe this much." She pinched her fingers together.

"I think a little more than that," Kieran smiled at her.

Tiana began grinding against Kieran's lap, anxious to feel him inside her. "Tyson is asleep," she said in a sing-song fashion.

Kieran briefly closed his eyes as he felt Tiana's movements against his lap. He was hard as steel and it was taking every bit of energy to not flip Tiana over on the couch and release her tension. But he knew his boundaries and if Tiana truly wanted him, she would proposition him when she's sober. "I need to put you to bed, Tiana," he softly spoke.

Tiana softly kissed Kieran's neck, emitting a low moan from him. "Do you want to come with me?" She whispered.

Kieran briefly closed his eyes as Tiana continued to kiss his neck and grind against him. Oh, he wanted to bed her, alright. But he had another idea in mind; something they both wouldn't regret. "Sure," Kieran motioned for Tiana to stand up and he followed her to her bedroom. She began to undress in front of him. "Let me go take care of some business and I'll be right back."

"Sure thing, baby," Tiana took off her shirt and yoga pants, revealing a toned body. "I'll be waiting."

Kieran stared a long time at Tiana's figure. Her body was shaped like an hourglass that was just out of control. Her breasts were full, not too big and not too small. They would fit perfectly in his hands and mouth. Her thighs were thick and she had a bit of a tummy but it accentuated her body. Kieran already imagined what positions he would twist Tiana's body in and he quickly had to put a lid on the rising nature of his cock.

He rushed out of her bedroom and went to the bathroom to splash some cold water on his face. He looked at himself in the mirror and just wondered how drunk *he* had to be to pull off the next stunt. He couldn't tell his brothers about this at all. They would never let him live it down.

Kieran returned to Tiana's bedroom a short while later and found her naked and passed out. He softly kissed her forehead as he covered her body with a blanket. Kieran glanced at Tiana one last time before leaving her bedroom. He was determined the next time he was going to tuck her into bed, it would be after they finished making love.

FIVE

Oh...so dizzy...what...what day is it?

Tiana stumbled out of bed as she tried figure out why on Earth she had to finish that entire bottle of wine last night. And by herself, to boot! She was fortunate she chose to get blitzed on a Friday night. There was no way she would've been able to go to work in the condition she was in.

She went to the bathroom and freshened herself up. She looked at herself in the mirror and couldn't believe the sight. Dark circles encompassed her eyes and there was a little crust in the inner corners. Her normally pressed hair was stringy and looked like awful bedhead. She had brief reminders of her youth, when she would party into dawn with her college roommates and return home sometime before noon.

But she was young, dumb, and full of cum back then, some fifteen years prior. She was currently 32, intelligent, and well, she had never been in a drought so long like she currently was.

The prior night...it was fuzzy. Things were clear when Kieran arrived home but it got blurry when he sat next to her on the couch. They talked...yes, they talked. They laughed and kidded around about something. And then...*oh God...*

Tiana gasped at the memory. She propositioned Kieran. She climbed on top of him and...she couldn't quite remember what happened after that. She was naked, though. Something *did* happen. Did they make love? Why couldn't she remember that? She would've remembered *that*, right?

Tiana was getting dizzy again just thinking about everything. She managed to put her long mane into a ponytail and rushed into Tyson's nursery. He was gone but there was a note in his crib.

I took him with me today. You looked like you needed your rest.

Kieran.

Tiana jumped in the shower and scrubbed her body clean. She dried off and hurriedly put some clothes on. She practiced how she was going to approach Kieran. Should she be casual about it? No, that would be awkward. Maybe she should be strictly professional with him, as if he was one of her colleagues? No, she would come off as if what happened last night didn't mean anything.

Maybe she could be lovey-dovey with him? No, she wasn't sure if that was appropriate since Kieran clearly didn't spend the night. The thought just occurred to her. Why didn't he spend the night? Was she that bad in bed? Did he not like her body? Did she hog the covers? Did she snore?

Tiana rushed out the door to Kieran's home. She was going to settle everything once and for all. If they made love, she needed to know how to approach him and not compromise their working relationship. It was the best course of action.

Tiana walked over to Kieran's home and knocked on the door. She heard grunting and shuffling from the outside. *Am I interrupting something?*

Kieran appeared at the front door a short time later. He was sweaty and out of breath. "Tiana," he greeted her, "Good Morning."

Tiana looked at the god before her and momentarily stopped breathing. A hand clutched her necklace and she lightly wetted her lips. Kieran was shredded. His ebony hair was lightly wet and brushed against his shoulders. Sweat beaded against his tawny skin and his nipples were erect. Was that an eight-pack he had? She quickly counted. It was. How was that even possible?

Tiana imagined flicking her tongue on his nipples as she straddled his body, his cock pressing against her thighs as she slowly lowered onto his body, taking all of him at once and...

"Is everything okay, Tiana?" Kieran asked.

Tiana shook her head to relieve her thoughts. "Oh yes. Everything is fine." She cleared her throat. "I was just wondering what you were up to."

"I was just finishing up a workout while Tyson is taking a power nap." Kieran wiped his brow with the back of his hand. "What's up?"

"I just wanted to know if you wanted to come over for dinner later. I'm making spaghetti. I'm sure it won't be as great as your mother's but it'll be a close second, I hope." Tiana offered an olive branch.

"I would love to," Kieran smiled. "Just let me finish up here and I'll be right over."

"Cool," Tiana glanced down at her feet, "um, I wanted to talk to you about what happened last night?"

"Tiana, it's cool." Kieran smiled. "Nothing happened. I tucked you in bed and left. I picked up Tyson this morning because I had a feeling you wouldn't be able to."

Tiana wasn't sure if she was relieved or embarrassed. "Thank you."

"You're welcome," Kieran flashed his warm smile again.

"Um," Tiana wasn't sure how to approach the next topic on her mind. "About my clothing..."

"It's fine," Kieran replied, "I didn't see anything I wasn't supposed to see."

Tiana felt her shoulders drop. Kieran didn't see her naked. She couldn't understand why she felt disappointed. "Good to know. Well, I guess I better get going and start that spaghetti."

"Okay. I'll see you in about an hour?" He asked.

"Sure," Tiana tightened her lips. An hour wasn't nearly enough time but she could work miracles like she always had. "I'll see you later." She left Kieran's home a short time later. She didn't know why or even how her legs started running as fast as they did but she found herself sprinting back to her home.

****

"Wow," Kieran's nose was tickled with mouth-watering aromas when he entered Tiana's home. "This is very nice."

Tiana wasn't sure how she was able to do it but she managed to pull off a meal of salad, spaghetti, and garlic bread within her hour timeframe. Thank goodness for easy to follow directions on the packages. "It's nothing, really," she half-lied. "Have a seat and relax."

Kieran put Tyson down in rocking crib chair and made himself a seat at the bar as he watched Tiana in action. He wanted to be honest with her about what really happened the night before; how he admired her body and lusted after her just as much—if not more—as she wanted him. Her body was incredible and he couldn't take his mind off the different positions he wanted to put her in. He'd never worked out so hard in his life, trying to get his mind off her.

But the embarrassment in Tiana's eyes told Kieran she was not interested in him in that manner. She was drunk off her tail and her inhibitions were gone. She saw him as her employee and that was that.

If only he could get the thought out of his mind; of him kissing every part of her naked body, then nestling himself between her thighs as her tight heat welcomed him and…

"Kieran?" Tiana called his name again. "Did you want a soda? Water?"

Kieran's thoughts snapped him back to the present. "Sure, I'll have a soda. Thank you."

Tiana poured soda in a couple of glasses for both Kieran and herself. "So," she began, "you never did tell me about the personal drama in your past."

Kieran clinked glasses with Tiana and took a sip. "Not much to tell. I was married once before; high-school sweetheart. Got married straight out of high school. We just eloped, went to Atlantic City, and came back to tell our parents."

"How did your mom take it?" Tiana asked.

"Not well." Kieran remembered how his mother started cursing in Italian while clutching her rosary and shouting at the ceiling, begging for God to forgive her son and his foolishness. At the time he was embarrassed. Looking back on it, he was rather amused at the dramatics his mother went through. "But she quickly got over it once she realized I didn't get Jalara knocked up."

"So you got married young but you're not married now," Tiana knew she was stepping into dangerous territory but she had to know. "What happened?"

"I did a tour and came back to a cleaned-out apartment and bank accounts." Kieran shook his head. Jalara was the love of his life.

After much soul-searching, he realized she was with him because he had money and not necessarily because of any love. "I was smart enough to not have her on my credit card accounts or she would've maxed out those cards as well. So yeah…"

Tiana instinctively reached out and grabbed Kieran's hand. "I'm so sorry to hear that."

Kieran squeezed Tiana's hand. "Everything happens for a reason. Maybe things had to fall apart so better things can come together."

A sensual air passed between them as their eyes locked on each other and neither dared to let go of the other's hand. Once again, Tiana felt the same electricity zap through her body as before. She was convinced it was from having her arm directly over the stove. "Lunch will be ready soon."

Six

"You know what I rather be doing?" Tiana asked.

"What would you rather be doing?" Her attorney, Marcus Russell, replied.

"Anything but this."

Tiana and Marcus were in a mediator's office waiting for Christopher and his counsel. A civil agreement between the exes flew out the window the moment Christopher decided to contest the iron-clad prenuptial agreement between him and Tiana. He claimed he was of unsound mind when he signed the document, despite evidence to the contrary.

Nevertheless, Tiana found herself embroiled in a fight over her fortune. She only wished Christopher had the same energy towards their son. Christopher used to wine and dine her; spoil her senseless with the shopping sprees and spontaneous trips somewhere. She had the bling, the Blahniks, and the baller.

She also had the bullshit, the heartache, and was the laughing stock amongst her friends and outsiders. Every industry party she attended, Christopher would flirt with another woman right in front of Tiana. There were plenty of rumors of side pieces in major metropolitan cities. And Tiana could never forget the paternity claim that was disproven.

No man was worth giving up her self-worth, ever again. While her soul wanted to be that 70's flower child that she craved, her everyday appearance was definitely not that.

"Marcus, nice to see you here," Christopher's attorney, Sammy Lawford, entered the office with Christopher in tow.

"Pleasure to see you, Sam," Marcus shook hands with him. "I hope we can be quick about this."

"I believe we can," Sammy sat down and Christopher sat next to him.

Christopher stared at his ex-wife who was working on a presentation for a new client she acquired over the past several weeks. Her hair was wrapped tight in a bun and her makeup was impeccable. She wore a grey suit with pearl jewelry. She looked everything like the goddess he met years ago at an industry function.

"Champagne Cris, my man!" A rapper, Young Thug, approached him and gave him a bro hug.

"What up, baby?" Christopher hugged the man back. "What's going on?"

"Nothing, nothing!" The young man let out a heavy sigh. His first single was burning up the charts and his debut album was just certified platinum, thanks to Christopher's heavy-hitting production. They were celebrating the album's success at a party just for Young Thug. "I owe all this to you, man! Without you, I couldn't have done any of this."

"Well, you know…I had the beats but you were the one with the talent," Christopher smiled. "I was just doing my job, man. That's all."

"I hear that, I hear that. Well, listen, let me go mingle with some people and I'll holler back at you. Later, dude!" He threw up the peace sign and walked off.

Christopher nodded with his cup full of Hennessey. He was proud to see up and coming young artists receive their due. He had been applauded by the industry for his eclectic producing style, often switching it up depending on who he worked with. He produced rock acts, country artists, and was the mastermind behind several hip-hop classic records. Champagne Cris was the man.

Christopher Schmidt was a lonely person.

He started creating beats when he was a child, as young as ten. He would beat-box into the microphone and play it back for his friends who would rap against the beat. As he grew older he spent much time in clubs, DJ-ing during the weekends and some weekday nights. His mother implored him to finish high school, but Christopher knew college wasn't in his future. He wanted to be a producer. He wanted to make classic records and beats like his idol, Dr. Dre.

He bought the latest equipment, sometimes spending a whole paycheck and forgoing groceries for the month. He would spend hours cultivating his craft, going over a stanza until it was perfect to his ears. He created mix-tapes and gave them away to anyone who cared. He didn't care about the money; he knew it was going to come. He just wanted to be known.

Several years later, Christopher finally got his big break. He was signed to a major label and created beats for their powerhouse artists. His overnight success actually took several years but it was all worth it once he got his first big check. He entertained the groupies and often slept with struggling female artists who couldn't afford his services but wanted to repay him in some way. But at the end of the night, he was alone. He woke up alone, he ate alone, and he slept alone. "I'm tired of this shit," Christopher muttered to himself.

"Tired of what? We just got here." Christopher's brother and manager, Dean, stood beside him.

"Nah, not the party, man." Christopher shook his head. "I'm tired of being alone."

"Being alone?" Dean was incredulous. "Didn't I just see you with three different women last week?"

"No, I'm not talking about those chickenheads I mess with. I'm talking about a woman. A real woman. Someone who can season a chicken and not roll a blunt. She probably wouldn't know what a blunt is." Christopher fantasized. "I'm talking about someone who can be my freak in the sheets and a lady in the streets."

"Yeah, those chicks don't exist, bro," Dean said apologetically. "I have yet to meet one."

Christopher looked up and saw the most beautiful woman he had ever seen in his life. She was lithe and wearing a dress so tight, it appeared to be painted on her body. She had long flowing hair—it looked real and her own, not a weave. Her lips sparkled with a nude lipstick and her eyes danced whenever someone greeted her.

Christopher was already in love and determined to have her. "Nah, they exist," Christopher determined. "I'm sure of it. Excuse me for a minute, bro." Christopher walked up to Tiana and introduced himself. "Hello, there."

"Hello," Tiana smiled back.

"How are you doing tonight? I noticed you were alone." Christopher asked.

Tiana looked back at the man before her. He was White, thick around the waist, and his mouth boasted of shiny grills. She would later find out the grills were platinum. He had his brown hair cropped close to his head and a light beard and goatee. He had inquisitive brown eyes and a seductive tone.

He wore a long platinum chain and was a walking advertisement for several stores, based on all of the name brands he was sporting. Despite his interesting looks, the man was attractive. "I'm doing just fine and I'm just here temporarily to say hi to Steven and then I'll be on my way."

"Steven?" Christopher asked.

Tiana shook her head. "I'm sorry. Young Thug." She corrected. "I was his financial advisor and he invited me to his platinum sales party, so I'm just here to let him know I came, and then I'll be on my way."

Christopher was already in love. Tiana wasn't like any woman he had ever met. "You're a financial advisor, huh?"

"Yes. I have my own business." Tiana met eyes with Young Thug and waved at him. "Excuse me for a minute, I need to go say hello. It was a pleasure talking to you…"

"Christopher. My name is Christopher."

"Pleasure talking to you, Christopher." Tiana shook hands with him. "I hope to talk to you again, soon."

"I don't know your name," Christopher pleaded.

"Tiana," she smiled, then left.

Christopher watched Tiana give Young Thug a hug as he introduced her to other people in his entourage. Christopher was determined that by the end of the night, Tiana was going to leave with him.

"I'm sorry I have to run, Steven, I have an early morning tomorrow. But I wanted to stop in and say hello and congratulate you on your success." Tiana grinned.

"Hey, if it wasn't for you, I would be broke already like these other no-name rappers out here," Young Thug laughed. "Thanks for keeping me focused."

"Not a problem, Steven." Tiana kissed his cheek. "I'll see you later."

Tiana walked away from Steven and out of the party. It was almost ten p.m. and the night was still young but, as the president and CEO of Morris Financial, she had no choice but to turn in early. No one was going to run her business for her, despite how much she wanted a clone. Tiana had to remind herself, however, that there was no rest for the wicked. Good things come to those who wait, but she also knew those who work for it got better results and more satisfaction.

She gave the valet her ticket and waited for her car. It was starting to get a little chilly in the autumn air and she covered her arms with her wrap. "So you have any plans for tonight?" Christopher walked up beside her.

Tiana turned towards him and grinned. "Yes, I'm going home."

"The night is still young," he glanced down at his watch, "it's only 9:30."

"I have a really early morning tomorrow. I have to be in my office by five a.m." Tiana yawned, "I shouldn't even be here right now. It's way past my bedtime."

"Oh well, I was hoping to convince you to go to a little jazz club down the street from here if you're not really into hip-hop music."

"I'm into the old stuff, not so much the new." Tiana confessed. "I can't name one new rapper."

"The old stuff is always better," Christopher licked his lips. "Anyway, I'm not going to keep you but here's my card if you're interested." He handed Tiana a business card.

Tiana studied Christopher's card. "Champagne Cris, huh?"

"Yeah, you might have heard of me?" He winked.

"Yeah, I have." Tiana's Prius pulled up to the sidewalk.

"What do you think?"

"You were right," Tiana yelled out to him before she entered her car, "the old stuff is always better."

Christopher jumped back into the present. He should've known that night what a bitch his ex-wife would've become. "Let's proceed, shall we?"

****

"This is nice, huh?" Kieran asked Tyson. "Just nature and us bros, huh?"

Kieran took Tyson to a nearby park for a picnic date. He laid out a blanket and had a picnic basket full of healthy food for them both: pureed pears and peas for Tyson, and a bagged lunch for himself. The October air was warm with a slight breeze; it was officially fall and leaves from the trees were already on the ground.

Kieran particularly liked the fall season; it always reminded him of his birthday. Ever since he was little, his mother always made a big deal about birthdays. He could remember seeing all of his friends and family gathering around the table as he made a wish and blew out candles. It was always a big celebration with plenty of food, music, and laughter to last for days. There was never enough money for gifts but Kieran didn't care. All he ever wanted was waiting for him in Staten Island.

It just occurred to Kieran his birthday was coming up in a few weeks. He was going to ask Tiana if he could possibly take a few days off so he could go back to Staten Island and celebrate with his family. As he fed Tyson, Kieran thought of a better idea. He was going to ask Tiana if she wanted to join him. She could bring Tyson and all three of them could stay at his mother's home.

Kieran wiped Tyson's mouth and began to burp the infant. The more he thought about the idea, the better it sounded. He was a bit curious on the sleeping arrangements. He and Tiana were not a couple, at least not yet. His mother's home had four bedrooms and one of his brothers still lived at home. He could probably sleep in one room and kick Tony out of his room so Tiana and Tyson could sleep there. Or maybe they could get a hotel room with two beds and a crib.

The thought made Kieran uncomfortable. He would be damned if he was going to get a hotel room with a woman he was in love with and not sleep with her. In love? No, he wasn't in love. He was in heavy infatuation. It sounded better. It was more than lust but not quite being in love. Heavy infatuation. It sounded like a fancy dinner. Oh, I'll have the heavy infatuation, please?

Now if he believed it, it would be true.

****

"You look like you could use a drink," Allison appeared at the doorway to her boss's office.

Tiana took off her blazer and threw it onto another chair. The divorce proceedings were long and Christopher and his attorney fought pretty much every single point Tiana and her attorney brought up. That didn't make her heated, though. What really made Tiana almost stand on top of the conference table and wind her leg back so she could get a good, swift kick to Christopher's jaw was the fact he didn't want anything to do with Tyson. Still, Christopher was smart enough to stop short of signing off his rights. He knew if Tiana suddenly died, Tyson would become one very rich boy. He eventually signed off on the papers and in a few months, Tiana would be a free woman.

"I'm never getting married again," Tiana sighed. "Never."

"Never say never," Allison was a hopeless romantic.

"Never, never, never, never, ever, ever, ever," Tiana retorted. "Ever."

Allison laughed. "You say that now but once you meet The One…"

"I thought I met The One and look how that turned out?" The mediation ended over two hours prior to Tiana going to work, however, it took her just as long to calm down. "I'm done with marriage. I'm done with dating. Done, done, done."

Allison held up her hands in defense. "Okay, no need to convince me," she handed Tiana her mail. "You have a few things in the mail today, including the invitation to the charity auction."

"Shoot!" Tiana huffed. "I totally forgot about that. I guess I need to figure out what I'm going to wear."

"And don't you need to figure out who's your date?" Allison smiled.

Tiana wasn't amused by her assistant. "I think you have some work to do."

"How was your day?" Kieran greeted Tiana with a hug.

"Hectic and dramatic," Tiana smiled. It was nice coming home to Kieran. He seemed to relieve any problems she had whenever she saw him. "I'm really glad I live a boring life."

"You keep saying you have a boring life and I just don't see it," Kieran offered Tyson to her.

"Because it is boring," Tiana bounced Tyson on her hip. "I work all day and come home to my son. I also deal with the occasional B.S. from my ex but that's to be expected."

Kieran hesitated on his next thought. He wanted to ask Tiana how that morning's divorce proceedings went. He knew if they went well, he might be out of a job soon. With shared custody of Tyson, there would be no reason for Tiana to keep Kieran. His feelings were a reason why he always sent his employees out to do assignments. He didn't want to become attached to the families. If only he could wear his emotions on his sleeve like his brothers.

"But don't worry about us," Tiana seemingly read Kieran's mind, "you'll be around for a long while. And that's a fact."

Kieran breathed a small sigh of relief. He felt the constricting grip loosen around his heart. It was then he knew there was more to just him wanting to stay and watch over Tyson. He wanted to watch over Tiana as well. "I'm always here to help," was his only response.

"This weekend, I have a dinner I'm going to. It's a boring, high-society affair. Black-tie type of thing," Tiana began.

"Sounds like a good time," Kieran gave a warm smile.

"Meh. You've been to one; you've been to them all. Anyway, I was wondering if you want to come with me?" She asked. "I don't like attending these things alone. I can always ask one of my friends to watch Tyson. It wouldn't be any trouble at all." Tiana felt her mouth was going at the same speed of her pounding heart.

"I would love to go," Kieran smiled, "when is it?"

"It's on Saturday," Tiana added, "we'll have a car pick us up and then we'll be on our way."

"I look forward to it," Kieran smiled. It wasn't a date but it was the next best thing.

****

She wasn't planning on spending her Saturday afternoon like this.

Tiana stood in front of the dressing room mirror in her walk-in closet and stared at herself. Her arms were flabby and reminded her of chicken wings. Her thighs looked like hammocks. Her stomach wasn't as toned as it used to be. There were still leftover stretch marks from her pregnancy.

She examined her face. She hated her acne scars and probably should invest in a dermatologist. Her nose was a bit wide. Okay, she should invest in a plastic surgeon as well. Her lips, oh God, her lips were so full and plump. They reminded her of when she was younger and how the boys would tease her because of her full lips. Little did she realize as she grew older, men would salute them.

Tiana was a nervous wreck. She'd asked Kieran out not thinking he would actually accept. To her shock, he did and he was looking forward to it. Why in the hell did he have to accept? Did he not realize the tizzy he put her in? What if he expects her to put out? What if he's bored? What if he quits the next day?

Tiana put aside her racing mind. She finally decided on a tight red dress. It gave her the appearance of being skinny and would take the attention off her flaws. She put her hair up in a French roll and did her makeup. She splashed three sprays of perfume and headed out the bathroom.

Oh, her foolish heart.

She was putting on the finishing touches when she heard her front door open. "Tiana? I'm here," Kieran called out.

"I'm almost ready," Tiana yelled back, "I'll be down in about five minutes."

Kieran's lips curved into a smile. Tiana might have said five minutes but he knew how women operated. Five minutes to them was the equivalent of an hour. He might as well get comfortable.

He walked over to the kitchen and looked for vases. He managed to find a couple of them underneath the sink. He rinsed off one vase and placed the roses inside. He arranged the flowers the way his mother and his brother, Joey, taught him. "In case that child care thing doesn't work out," Joey once told his older brother, "you can always come back and help us out at the floral shop."

Kieran had just finished arranging the roses when Tiana appeared in his sight. "Well, hello there…" she smiled.

Kieran looked over at Tiana and felt air escape his lips. She was absolutely stunning. Her makeup was impeccable and the dress tightly hugged her body. She was lightly fragranced with notes of floral, patchouli, and vanilla.

Kieran grabbed a single rose from the vase and handed it to her. "You look absolutely breathtaking."

Tiana sniffed the pink rose and smiled. She'd truly forgotten how nice it was to receive flowers. Christopher barely gave her any. Hell the fool barely remembered her birthday, despite it being in the same week as his. For a brief moment, Tiana was annoyed. How could she have stayed with him for so long?

Her thoughts finally turned to something pleasant—her date for the evening. Kieran didn't opt for a tuxedo and instead wore a business suit with an open collar. The outfit was simple but his body was tailor-made for it. His cologne was a combination of earth, wood, and musk.

Tiana felt her heart beat…pound, really. She swallowed again and her tongue darted out to quickly wet her lips. Tiana blinked twice and let out a small breath. The heat pooling between her thighs spread throughout her body. She always found Kieran attractive but it was at that moment she realized she was *attracted* to him. She may not have been in love with Kieran—not yet—but she was definitely in lust with him.

That was a new feeling for her. She didn't want to just see him naked. She wanted his body to hover over her, sliding his cock in and out as she opened wider to accommodate him and…

"Tiana? Is everything okay?" Kieran asked.

Tiana jumped back to the present. "Yes," she smiled. "I was lost in a train of thought."

"Want to share?" He offered.

Just as Tiana was contemplating what plausible lie she could think of, the doorbell rang. The chauffeur had arrived. "Time to go."

 It was going to be a long night.

SEVEN

"Tiana!" Her colleague, Benjamin Li, greeted her with a polite hug. "I'm glad to see you here!"

"Nice to see you, Ben. Where's Virginia?" Tiana inquired about his wife.

"Fixing her dress for the umpteenth time," Ben rolled his eyes. "I told her to not wear something so damn tight, but what do I know? I'm just a husband and she's just a wife spending my money."

Ben was an older Asian gentleman with salt and pepper hair and a thin build. He was usually stoic and his employees thought his lips were permanently sealed. To see him smile was rare and to hear a laugh was quite impossible. Ben did laugh and smile, however, when he was liquored up. Then he became delightful.

"You're a very patient man, Ben," Tiana smiled.

"It's because of this," Ben waved his glass full of bourbon.

"Happiness in a glass," Kieran commented.

"You're goddamn right," Ben raised his glass.

"I'm sorry, where are my manners?" Tiana shook her head. "Ben, this is my date, Kieran."

"Nice to meet you, Kieran," Ben shook his hand. "So what do you do?"

"I'm in early education services," Kieran gave the standard, canned response he always gave when someone inquired about what he did for a living. It was better than explaining why a grown man was a nanny.

"Early education services?" Ben nodded approvingly. "What's that?"

"I own and operate a child care business."

"That must be lovely," Ben took another sip, "being around a bunch of screaming little maggots all day."

"Well, it's not that bad…"

"And I bet their parents are a piece of work! They're probably just as bad as those screaming maggots they're dropping off. Absentee father who's fucking every stupid and impressionable eighteen-year-old he would get a stiffy for. And the mother whose face is so pulled back, it actually takes away from the obvious distraction of the giant stick up her ass." Ben took another sip, finishing his drink. "Excuse me, I need a refill. Open bar tonight, brah. Go getcha one."

"Will do," Kieran smiled before Ben left. "He was entertaining."

"It's because he's drunk," Tiana led Kieran to another bar, "He's normally not like that."

"There's nothing wrong letting loose every once in a while. Letting your inhibitions free."

Tiana thought about the other night when she propositioned Kieran. She was still embarrassed by what happened. He saw her naked but didn't comment one way or another about it. That bothered Tiana more than she would've liked. "For some people," she added.

Kieran held Tiana's waist and leaned in to her. "For everyone," he whispered.

There went that flushed feeling again. Tiana was convinced she was getting hot flashes.

****

"And next on the auction block is a pair of Lakers tickets, floor row for three games this season. That is any game you want to go to, including playoff games," The auctioneer announced, "we'll start the bidding at ten thousand dollars."

"Are you interested?" Tiana asked Kieran. "Football's more my thing. I'm waiting for the forty-niner tickets to go up."

Kieran glanced at Tiana. Was she a woman after his heart? "Are you serious?"

"I love football! I like basketball too, but football is more my thing." Tiana commented.

"Let's wait for the football tickets," Kieran put an arm around Tiana and she leaned into him. "I won't mind."

"Going once? Going twice? Sold to the man in the back! Please see the cashier for the arrangements, sir." The auctioneer announced.

Tiana turned around to see who won and was pleasantly surprised to see one of her clients and longtime friends. "Excuse me, Kieran. I need to say hello real quick." She left for the cashier's table.

Tiana stood at a respectable distance until the business transaction was completed and then approached her good friend. He was impeccably dressed in a business suit and open collar. He looked every bit of the multimillionaire he was. "I wondered if I'd see you here tonight."

Scott Reed turned around and gave Tiana a big hug. "Tiana, great to see you!" He kissed her cheek. "How have you been?"

"I've been well, how have you been?"

"Oh, I've been doing fine. Things are finally stabilizing so no complaints here," he smiled.

Tiana motioned towards the auction room where Scott's date was sitting. She was a Black female with long, straight hair and wearing a body-hugging black gown. "I bet," she grinned, "fling or girlfriend?"

"Girlfriend. Her name is Mari." Scott replied to Tiana's surprise, "I know, huh?"

"There's nothing wrong with monogamy," Tiana kidded.

"Everyone keeps telling me that," Scott shrugged, "I don't know why."

"Maybe it's because deep down you're the monogamous type?"

"Maybe," Scott smiled, "but I see you didn't come alone yourself."

"Oh, Kieran?" Tiana turned back to him and a smile formed on her face. Even from a distance, she missed his company. "He's a great guy."

"He better be," Scott politely warned.

"I know you're not trying to be Mr. Protective over me?" Tiana folded her arms.

"I'm protective of all of my female friends," Scott added, "even those that reject me."

"I didn't reject you," Tiana scoffed, "it just wasn't the right time for us." It was a time when Scott just ended a disastrous relationship and Tiana was working double to get her investment firm off the ground. She often wondered what would've happened if they both simply waited just a few more months…*Right love, wrong time.*

"Coulda, woulda, shoulda," Scott shrugged as he grabbed his tickets, "at least we have MBA memories."

While they both were studying for their Master's degrees at USC, they often took sex breaks with each other that would last for hours. Even when she was with Christopher, she would fantasize it was Scott on top of her, commanding her body in various positions. Even momentarily, she thought about how big and thick he was and how he somehow managed to fit into her tight heat over and over again.

He was some dick she would never forget. "The MBA program was awesome," Tiana smiled and gave her friend a hug and a kiss, "I'll see you later, Scott. We need to talk soon about your latest acquisition of the nightclub."

"Sure thing, Tiana. See you later," he replied.

After the charity auction, Tiana walked outside to the balcony of the Ritz-Carlton. She inhaled a sharp breath and admired the city lights. She had come a long way from being a bright-eyed, big-idea girl from the suburbs to living in a mansion in Pacific Palisades. Her family appeared to be the modern-day Huxtables. Her father, Henry, was a respected oncologist. Her mother, Barbara, was a hairstylist. Tiana was an only child.

They were strict parents, encouraging Tiana to follow her dreams and not get caught up in the streets like some of their peers. Tiana could remember how much she hated living with her parents. They never let her do anything without Tiana giving them a list of who was going to be with her, where they were going, and what was going to take place. Nowadays, she could appreciate why they acted the way they did.

But with everything good, there was some bad. Barbara was determined to not have her daughter be a 'fat one' and put Tiana on a strict diet when she was an adolescent, eating nothing but carrots and celery sticks to drop her cherub cheeks. Henry encouraged Tiana to go into occupations that would make her the most money, regardless if she had a passion for it. When Tiana expressed an interest in becoming a doula, her parents scoffed at her decision, encouraging her to become a doctor instead. Luckily for Tiana, she also had a strong interest in financial affairs and became an accountant, much to the satisfaction to her parents.

Stuck. That's the word she was looking for. She felt stuck in her life. She was always supposed to do something right. There was always an insanely high level of expectation on her. She was always supposed to do the right thing with the right guy with the right life. Tiana finally conceded her life was just as bland as her diet. The only thing that jolted her every now and then was the acrimonious divorce from Christopher. His last demand was laughable at best—give him twenty-five million and he'll go away forever. He never once mentioned seeing Tyson.

"I was looking for you," Kieran approached her from behind.

Tiana slightly turned to him and gave a half-grin. "Hey," she rubbed her shoulders in the cool October breeze.

"Oh, come on," Kieran placed his drink on the balcony and took off his blazer. He covered Tiana's bare shoulders with it. "I can't be that bad of a date, am I?"

Tiana bundled herself up a little more with the blazer. "Just curious," she turned to him, "I don't have a giant stick up my ass, do I?"

"What?" Kieran smiled.

"I thought about what Ben said earlier, about the child care parents. I mean, what he said about my ex was true but I'm wondering if he grouped me in there," she frowned.

"You honestly believe that?"

"I admit I can be a bit stuffy. I'm paid to be," Tiana shrugged. "If I was who I truly am, I wouldn't get any clients. I definitely wouldn't have any respect."

"So who is the real Tiana?"

"Will the real Tiana Morris please stand up?" She chuckled. "She's fun and free-spirited. She's organizational to a fault but not stuffy. She loves going to the opera, just as much as she loves watching Football Sunday, just as much as she loves seeing the latest chick flick. If she could, she would wear her natural, kinky and curly hair all the time and do away with those flat irons and god-forsaken relaxers. She would love to expand her family, having lots of babies to fill up that big-ass house she bought."

Kieran admired Tiana's honesty. For the first time, the real came through. There was no alcohol, no contriteness, no keeping up with appearances. The real Tiana was with him. It was refreshing and wonderful. "So why does that Tiana stay hidden?"

"Because *that* Tiana won't get any respect. *That* Tiana will lose millions in potential investments from clients all over. *That* Tiana…" she paused and bit her lip.

"You were saying?" He encouraged.

Tiana cleared her throat and exhaled a deep breath. "*That* Tiana is afraid of what her family would think. And she has to keep prim and proper. So *that* Tiana stays hidden."

Kieran moved closer to her and wrapped an arm around her. His embrace was warm and comforting. "I would like to see *that* Tiana if she wants to come out to play sometime."

Tiana humored him. "You wouldn't like her."

"How would you know that?"

"Because I do," she replied, curtly. "*That* Tiana comes with a whole lot of baggage. I'm not talking a few suitcases. I'm talking a 747."

"We all have baggage, Tiana," he offered.

"Easy for you to say," she scoffed.

"Oh?" Kieran accepted her challenge. "I hardly saw my mother while growing up. She always worked two or three jobs. I was the mother *and* the father to my brothers. When I got home from school, I had to make sure the house was clean, dinner was ready, and feed and bathe my younger brothers before I could even think about starting my homework and sometimes I didn't start my homework until it was damn near my bedtime.

"I joined the Army, fought a war on grounds I'm still not entirely clear about, and came home to find my high school sweetheart had cleaned me out and had taken everything but my clothing and shoes. We had a joint account of over ten grand; and there was about thirty cents left in there when I returned. It was two years before I got back on my feet and got my degree. So please, don't talk to me about baggage." Kieran clarified.

Tiana looked up at him with watery eyes. "I knew you wouldn't understand me!" She hurried to another corner.

Kieran quickly followed her. "I didn't say that to make you upset, Tiana, and I'm sorry. I said that to prove a point that yes, you may have baggage but so do I," he lifted her chin to his gaze and thumbed away her falling tears. "And I'm willing to go the distance with you if you let me."

"You're my nanny, Kieran," Tiana sniffled, "I'm not supposed to date the help."

"Would it make a difference if I was some random guy down the street? Some dude you met in a club?"

"Actually, yes," Tiana nodded and Kieran rolled his eyes. "I have a child, Kieran. I have a ready-made family. Not a lot of guys want to date a single mother. I'm a chance no one wants to take, no matter how much money I have."

"You're right, a lot of guys don't want to date a single mother," he captured her lips with his. She tasted sweetly of cinnamon and champagne. "But this guy wants his chance."

Kieran's lips were full and experienced and his mouth was so welcoming. Kieran slid his tongue inside Tiana's mouth and she met him halfway. It was rough, smooth, and inviting. "My life is going to be cute school plays, soccer games, orange slices, and PTA meetings in the future," she breathed. She felt her heart pounding in her chest and her breath was jagged. "Evenings like this would be rare."

"I like my quiet Saturday nights," he smiled.

"There will be times when I'll travel for weeks and won't be able to see you or Tyson." Kieran's lips trailed from her mouth and down her neck. Kieran made her feel like a woman again. A natural, warm-blooded, hot-bodied female with a healthy appetite for sex and a lot of it. She felt the forgotten moisture forming between her legs, her nipples sprang to attention, and the heat rose from her belly. It had been so long since she had been aroused; she'd almost forgotten what it felt like.

Kieran nibbled on her neck. His lips were hot, heavy, and wet. "I think we'll make do."

Her body craved him. Her heart *needed* him. She knew if they went home together, it would be the start of a new relationship. The ink on her divorce papers wasn't even dry yet. "I can't promise you anything, Kieran. I just got out of something and I'm not trying to get married again."

"All I need is your love," he held her close, "I'll take care of the rest."

Tiana pulled away from him. "It's been a long time, Kieran," she warned, "if we're going to go home and do what I hope we're going to do, I have to warn you, I'm rusty."

Kieran softly kissed Tiana again. "I'll lead."

****

"Do you want anything to drink?" Tiana kicked off her heels and headed to the kitchen. She'd purchased a refrigerator with a see-through door for the sole purpose of not wanting to open it up to see what was inside. "I have juice, filtered water, and champagne. I might have some liquor in the wet bar and…" Kieran appeared behind her and grabbed her waist. He kissed the back of her neck while his hands crawled up to her breasts and squeezed them. "Um…okay."

Kieran unzipped Tiana's dress and it fell to the floor. He admired the perfectly-rounded ass before him. He undid her bra and Tiana quickly covered her chest. "What's wrong, *bella*?"

"I'm ashamed of my breasts," Tiana admitted.

Kieran kissed her neck again, playfully nibbling on it. "Why? Your whole body is magnificent."

"I've always been flat in the chest area. I can barely fit a B cup."

"A B-cup isn't flat, Tiana," he replied.

"To me it is," she continued to cover them.

Kieran turned Tiana to face him. "I'll be the judge of that." He moved her arms from her chest and the bra fell down.

Tiana's eyes were squeezed shut. She couldn't bear to see the same level of disappointment Christopher gave her. He constantly suggested she get implants and she always refused. She hated how insecure he still made her.

She stayed still waiting for Kieran's disapproval. After a few quiet moments, she finally opened her eyes and saw Kieran looking back at her. His eyes were warm, thoughtful, and happy.

"You're gorgeous, Tiana. Absolutely gorgeous." Kieran's breath was jagged. He picked her up and carried her to the couch. He wanted to make love to her in a bed but he knew he couldn't wait that long. He laid her on the couch and quickly removed his clothing. Tiana's eyes widened upon seeing Kieran's cock. It was long, thick, and perfect. The slit was slightly wet with pre-cum and a hungry urge took over Tiana. Her tongue quickly darted over her dry lips. She was eager to feel him inside her mouth.

She grabbed his cock and slightly jerked it as she made eye contact with him. "Shit, Tiana..." Kieran moaned.

"Shh..." She quieted him before she took him in her mouth. Her mouth was hot and hungry, devouring his scent and taste. She sucked fast and hard, as if she couldn't get enough of him.

Kieran fisted Tiana's hair as he looked down at her. "*Bella*, I'm not going to be able to continue if you don't stop," he warned.

Tiana reluctantly stopped sucking Kieran and lay back on the sofa. Kieran crawled onto the sofa and hovered over Tiana. He captured her lips once again. Their tongues twirled and Tiana softly moaned in his mouth. He knew she wanted more.

He slid down her body, kissing her neck and her breasts. His mouth captured one breast and Tiana immediately arched in pleasure. Oh how wonderful it felt to have a man's lips on her body. He kissed her body slowly, exploring every curve, and reveling in her softness.

Kieran moved down Tiana's body and stopped at the beginning of her panties and playfully bit at them. He sat up, pulled them off her and tossed them in a corner. He nudged Tiana's thighs open and saw what he had been fantasizing about.

A single strip of hair covered her mound. Her chocolate folds glistened with desire. He nudged her thighs apart and saw her pink nub peek out. He put one thigh over his shoulders as he began to nibble on her clit. His tongue was quick—licking, tasting, and pleasing her as he held her down with his hands. Her back arched off the sofa and she softly moaned, thrusting upward to feel his tongue more.

She heard the familiar unwrapping of a condom and Kieran once again joined her on the sofa. He entered her and he immediately drew a sharp breath as she softly moaned. "Damn, Tiana," he whispered, "you feel like Heaven."

He hovered over her and he became hungry, greedy for her. He bent down to kiss her, to play with that curious tongue of hers. He moved faster inside her, his balls kissing her pussy with each hard thrust. He looked down at Tiana and saw her face. Her eyes were closed, her back was thrown back. She moaned, cried, begged…she needed that release. She needed to let go of that tension from her divorce, from her parents, from her life.

Kieran heard her mumble something along the lines of 'I'm about to cum' and he drove deeper inside her. When Tiana came, her whole body trembled and she clutched at his arms. "Kieran…Kieran, baby…" she breathed.

Tiana clenched tighter around Kieran's cock, encouraging him to finally cum. He exploded shortly afterward and stilled his body as the orgasm ran through him. "Tiana, my God, Tiana…" he moaned. He leaned down to kiss her once again. The kiss was slow and methodical; he wanted to savor every moment.

It was at that moment that Kieran realized he'd broken the cardinal rule of his child care business: never get too involved with the families. He wasn't just in over his head with Tiana; he was madly in love with her.

EIGHT

He never thought he would sleep in her bed.

Kieran had only been in Tiana's bedroom a handful of times. It was usually to get a toy for Tyson or put something away, but he never stayed longer than a few minutes. He felt he was invading Tiana's privacy and he wanted to keep her trust in him. The last time he was in her bedroom was to put her to bed after she drank herself into a lustful stupor. For weeks, Kieran wondered how drunk *he* must've been to not take advantage of her.

His patience paid off.

The rendezvous on the couch was the start of the night. They made love throughout the night, waking each other up with kisses and grabs. They had some funny moments when Tiana accidentally fell out of the bed during one of the positions or when Kieran would use character voices when he was on top of her, causing Tiana to laugh.

It was already one of his favorite memories.

He got up from bed and headed towards the kitchen to make some coffee. The previous night with Tiana was special, romantic, and powerful. Their bodies came together again throughout the night, tasting and taunting each other. Tiana's mouth was hungry and skillful as she repeatedly took Kieran's cock and sucked on it. Her heat was tight and welcoming, seemingly clutching his cock with every thrust he made. Her soft legs cradling his, encouraging him to fuck her faster and harder.

The night was perfect. Well, almost. When they switched positions and Kieran wanted Tiana on top, she would get on for a few minutes before she got off. "Let's do another position," she would nervously smile.

She was insecure, Kieran guessed. He would have to teach her not to be.

"You seem preoccupied," Tiana walked into the kitchen.

Kieran turned and smiled at her. Even with the bedhead and bare face, she was absolutely beautiful in the morning. "A little."

Tiana kissed him then walked over to the pantry. "What's on your mind? Tell me while I make us breakfast."

"You didn't want to get on top last night," Kieran revealed.

Tiana dropped the box of steel-cut oatmeal she was holding and it spilled over the floor. *He noticed that?* With all of the position changes, tangled sheets, and orgasms, Tiana didn't think too much of it. "Uh-huh."

"Is there a reason why?"

Great, now he wanted an explanation on top of noticing what she did. Why was it that the movies always had the morning after be so romantic and beautiful instead of the harsh reality of bullshit and bad breath?

She was about to get a broom to sweep the mess when Kieran beat her to the punch. "Allow me," he offered as he began to sweep.

Tiana looked down at him sweeping her floor. He was quiet and still waiting for an answer from her. She finally conceded and came clean. "I don't know how to ride," Tiana admitted.

Kieran cleaned up the floor and walked over to the trash can. "You don't know how to ride?" He emptied out the dust pan.

"Ride...ride..." Tiana felt her cheeks were on fire with embarrassment. "I don't know how to ride your penis."

A slow smile formed on Kieran's lips. He put away the broom and dust pan before proceeding to wash his hands at the kitchen sink. "Okay, um, Tiana, if you're going to talk dirty to me, you need to cut out the medical jargon."

Was it possible to become more embarrassed? Tiana thought so. She wanted to crawl underneath the deepest rock and stay there. "I never really talked dirty before."

"You just need to practice and let it roll off your tongue," Kieran approached her and snaked an arm around her waist. His lips lightly nibbled her ear while a free hand caressed her neck. "I can't wait to taste your pussy again. I love how tight you felt around my cock and you got so wet for me. I'm going to fuck you so hard, you're going to have bragging rights."

Tiana's tongue darted out to quickly moisten her lips. Kieran didn't just whet her appetite; he created a heat between her thighs that slowly spread throughout her body. She felt her pussy contract in anticipation. She swallowed a few times and let out a breath. "Um, that's nice..."

"Mmm..." Kieran moaned as his hands climbed up to Tiana's breasts. He softly squeezed them as he continued. "You want to give me that pussy again, don't you, *bella*?"

"Whew..." Tiana breathed. If she concentrated enough, she could possibly get the involuntary contractions her pussy was making to suddenly stop. How was it that he was able to make her want to get down on her knees and service him in just a matter of seconds? "I think I need a glass of water. Aren't you thirsty? I'm thirsty."

"Say it, Tiana," Kieran kept caressing Tiana's breasts as he softly kissed her neck, "tell me how much you want me."

Tiana closed her eyes and leaned into Kieran's body. "Yes…yes, baby."

"Say it, Tiana," Kieran whispered as he softly kissed her neck, "tell me how much you want me, *bella*. Tell how much you want me inside you. Tell me how much you want to put your legs on my shoulders."

Tiana took a few more breaths. Her lips slightly parted as a moan escaped. She was no longer aroused. She was just horny and wanted to fuck. No soft love-making, no sweet kisses and romantic music. There was no time for that shit. She wanted to be bent over the kitchen counter as she held onto anything that was nailed down.

"I want you to fuck me, baby," the words flowed out of her mouth, "I want you buried deep inside me."

Kieran pulled Tiana's top over her head and kissed the back of her neck, before trailing his lips down her bare back to the beginning of her pajama shorts. He slowly slid them off her waist and down her legs, kissing her ass and the back of her legs as he did it. He stood back up and bent Tiana over the counter. He spread her legs with his. "Don't move," he whispered to her before he left.

Tiana caught herself in the reflection of her glass door refrigerator. She never thought she would be so raw…so sexy. Kieran brought out a side in Tiana that was beyond freaky. She didn't know what it was, to be honest. All she knew was she liked it and couldn't get enough of it.

Kieran returned a short time later and quickly undressed. He tore open the condom wrapper and quickly slipped it on his hard cock. He stood directly behind Tiana and slid inside her, emitting a sharp breath from them both. "Steady, *bella*," Kieran moaned as she adjusted to his size. "Steady."

Tiana nodded as she gripped the counter harder. Kieran slowly began to move inside her and her pussy welcomed him with each stroke he gave her. His cock felt so thick, so wonderful, and there was no doubt she was addicted to him already. It seemed with each movement he made, the wetter she became, and she gripped him like a tight fist.

"Fuck, Tiana..." Kieran moaned as he moved faster inside her, his balls tickling her wet slit, "do you not know what you do to me? Do you not know?"

Tiana adjusted her position a little, slightly standing up as Kieran drove inside her. He had one hand firmly on her waist while the other one squeezed her breasts. She loved the way he filled her, her walls accommodating and pleasing him, encouraging him to fuck her faster, deeper, and forever. "Kieran, fuck me," Tiana begged him.

Kieran drove deeper and faster inside Tiana and she could no longer keep quiet. She used to be a silent lover, murmuring and whispering because it wasn't polite or ladylike. Deep, voracious moans escaped her lips. They started at the pit of her stomach and traveled up to her mouth, until she could no longer contain them.

Kieran wanted to fuck Tiana more, but his orgasm was approaching soon. "Are you about to cum? I don't know how much longer I can hold it off."

"Cum, baby," Tiana panted, "worry about me later."

Kieran held onto Tiana's hips as he came inside her, her pussy clenching and milking his cock. "Fuck, Tiana," he moaned as he kissed her sweat-covered back. He eased out of her and disposed of the condom. He then turned to Tiana and smiled. "Sit on the counter."

Tiana briefly looked back at the counter and then to Kieran. "I'm naked and wet, Kieran. I'm not sitting on the counter."

"Sit on it," he demanded, "I'm not repeating it."

Tiana was taken aback by Kieran's change in his voice. He demanded her to do something. It was dark, sexy, and authoritative. But what confused her was she was *turned on* by it. It had been a while since a man took control like that. Kieran was turning her out with each passing day.

Tiana sat on the counter and waited for his next instruction. Kieran walked over to her and kissed her lips, playing with her tongue. He then moved down to her breasts, with the dark cherry rosebuds at full attention. He licked and nibbled on them before he made his way to her heat. Her folds were still glistening and he could smell how intoxicating she was. Her clit was peeking out through the folds, begging to be licked and played with.

"Place your legs on my shoulders," Kieran instructed as Tiana complied. "Tell me when you're about to cum."

Kieran dipped his head to Tiana's pussy and began to lick it. Her pearl rolled around his tongue while a free hand spread her folds for easier access. His tongue was quick, making flicking motions on her clit.

Tiana squirmed and writhed beneath Kieran, wanting to ride his tongue. Her pussy began to contract again and Tiana knew she was going to cum. Her pussy was so hungry, so greedy for his tongue, his fingers, his cock, his hands…all of Kieran. Kieran's cock had filled her to the brink and now his tongue was going to send her over the edge. Her legs began to shake and the orgasm soon spread from her thighs to her belly to her chest to her face.

She screamed Kieran's name and pushed him away from her satisfied pussy. Her eyes were heavy-lidded and for a brief moment, Tiana forgot where she was.

Kieran picked up Tiana and carried her upstairs to her bedroom. He placed her on the bed and covered her with the sheets. He then joined her.

He'd teach her how to ride later that night.

****

"Girl, thank you for letting me watch Tyson," Erin gladly handed the infant back to Tiana, "you gave me a much-needed lesson on birth control. I almost forgot, so thank you."

"Oh, come on," Tiana cradled her son, "he wasn't that bad, was he?"

"He kept me up with his screaming and crying. I would put him down and he would cry like five minutes later. I would tend to him and everything would be fine for about ten minutes before he started wailing again. And then that smell from his diaper?" Erin gagged as she walked to the breakfast nook. "I still can't believe you let Cris hit that raw."

Tiana shushed her friend as she placed Tyson in her play pen. "You are so crude, Erin."

"I'm so honest, Tiana," Erin sassed back. "Anyway, did you have fun last night?"

"It was the same old boring gala I always go to," Tiana shrugged. She set a pot of tea on the stove and went to the pantry for snacks. "No big deal."

"Except you had a date this year," Erin winked. "I want all the details."

"There's nothing to say," Tiana felt her smile growing wider with each passing moment. She was already sore from last night but still craved more after what happened that morning. She tightened her lips before she turned back to her girlfriend. "We had a lovely time."

Erin tried to read Tiana's eyes to find a hint of what happened last night. There was nothing. She hated how stoic and plain Tiana could be if she didn't want anyone to read her. She was the queen of poker faces. "I bet you did," she snickered.

"I never talked about my sex life with Cris so what makes you think I'm going to reveal anything now?" Tiana placed an assortment of teas on the counter for Erin to choose from. "Make your choice."

"So did you just reveal something…?" Erin chose the raspberry tea.

"I didn't reveal a damn thing," Tiana smiled.

Erin read her best friend's eyes harder. Her eyes were still emotionless but there was a faint smile forming on her face. "He turned you out, didn't he?"

"You ask too many questions," Tiana set out the homemade cookies.

Erin glanced down at the homemade chocolate chip and walnut cookies. "You didn't make these, TeeTee."

"I've been learning how to cook, thank you very much." Tiana smiled.

Erin took a bite of a cookie. "These are delicious. Yeah, you definitely didn't make these," she chewed, "so he's great in bed and he can cook? All right, all right…"

"Will you be quiet with that noise?" Tiana looked back. She hoped Kieran didn't hear the conversation. "Nothing happened."

"Oh?" A slow smirk crawled on Erin's face. "We'll see about that when your man wakes up."

Tiana folded her arms. "What makes you think he spent the night here?"

The sound of a toilet flushing caused Erin to smile big. "Oh, I have my reasons…"

Kieran entered the kitchen a short time later. He kissed Tiana's cheek. "Hey Erin," he greeted her.

"Hey, *loverboy*," Erin winked. "Did you have a good time last night?"

"It was fun," Kieran walked over to the sink and grabbed a soapy sponge. He quickly wiped down the counter as he stole a glance at Tiana, who quickly covered her mouth with a hand. "It was a lot of fun."

Erin moved away from the counter to let Kieran clean it. "So are you two officially dating now?"

"You are really occupied with my personal life, Erin," Tiana replied.

"Because it's more interesting than mine." Erin quipped. She was in forced celibacy with her fiancée until they got married. She had done fine for the first three months, but with her wedding date soon approaching, she was starting to crack. She already broke two vibrators. "I'm occupied with anyone's sex life other than mine."

"You only have two more months," Tiana commented.

"Yeah, that's sixty days too damn long," Erin replied.

"There's nothing wrong with waiting," Kieran chimed in. "I waited for a while when I dated my first girlfriend."

"Oh yeah? How long did you wait?" Erin asked.

"Six months," Kieran shrugged. "If you really love someone, it's not a big deal. Besides, when it does happen, you'll be so glad you waited."

Erin smiled. Kieran gave her a new perspective. "I never thought of it like that before."

"It's easy to get caught up in wanting to get off like *now*." He offered. "But if you wait for the right moment, he'll still be screaming your name even when you're not together."

Erin got up from the counter. "And Tiana, you need to keep him." She grabbed another cookie. "I'll call you later, TeeTee."

"See you later, Erin," Tiana waved her out the door. She turned to Kieran. "I'm impressed."

"Oh?" Kieran took out Tyson's bath and put it in the sink.

Tiana picked up her son and began to undress him on the counter. "I've been trying to talk to her for months and she wouldn't listen. You talk to her for a few minutes and she finally quieted down. I'm impressed."

"It's because I'm a man," Kieran tested the water. "I don't offer the same advice that Cosmopolitan gives and honestly, no living and sane man—gay or straight—does. If you want advice on how to please a man, ask a man. Don't ask another woman. What may work for her may not work for you."

"You sound like you know your stuff."

"I've been around the block a few times," Kieran splashed a little water on Tyson.

"How many times?" Tiana inquired.

Kieran smiled at Tiana. "Really?"

"Really," Tiana smiled back. "I'm curious."

Kieran poured a little shampoo in his hands and began to wash Tyson's head. "What happened last night and this morning were from years of practice."

"More than both hands?"

Kieran raised an eyebrow. "Really?"

"I've had less than both hands," Tiana held up her hands. "What about you?"

"Let's put it like this," Kieran rinsed off Tyson's head, "I spent two years mending my broken heart on a weekly basis," he glanced back at Tiana, "so my number trumps yours by a *whole* lot."

Tiana smiled. "I'm glad you had so much practice," she kissed him.

"I would like to practice more tonight, if you want," he licked his lips.

"I have to be quiet this time," Tiana warned, "I can't be moaning and being loud with Tyson around."

"I wouldn't expect anything less," Kieran continued to bathe Tyson. "But I think you'll find it's a lot easier said than done."

"Ooh, is that a challenge?" Tiana licked her lips.

"I'm always up for a challenge, Tiana," Kieran's low rumble sent shockwaves through Tiana's core. "You talk a good game but we'll see if you could handle it."

"I can handle anything and everything," Tiana folded her arms.

"Good," Kieran dried off Tyson. "We'll see tonight, then."

****

"So, someone is all smiling and happy nowadays," Rocio stayed still as she got measurements on her bridesmaid dress. "Spill it, TeeTee."

"She ain't spillin' a damn thing! I already tried!" Erin huffed from her dressing room.

Tiana met up with her best friends for their fittings. Erin's wedding was rapidly approaching in a few months and the girls were doing last minute touch-ups. "What is there to talk about? Why can't I be private about my personal life?" Tiana tried on her bridesmaid dress.

"Because you're awfully quiet about a guy who likes you and you like him back," Rocio mentioned.

"I was just as quiet with Christopher, if I remember correctly," Tiana stepped out of the dressing room.

"After what he was doing to you, I would've been quiet about it, too." Erin answered from her room.

Rocio looked over at her best friend. "Can you spill the beans? I'm dying over here!"

"Fine," Tiana relented. She waited for the seamstress to leave the room. "I slept with Kieran."

"I knew it!" Erin shouted from the room. "I knew it when I went over that morning and had some cookies! Rocio girl, that man can cook!"

"So how did he like your cookies?" Rocio kidded.

"More importantly, were they dusty?" Erin added.

"He ate my cookie all night," Tiana reminisced. She could still feel how his tongue twirled on her swollen nub, lapping her up with every stroke. She wasn't just sprung on Kieran; she was in love with the man.

"That's what I'm talking about!" Erin walked out of her dressing room and revealed her A-line strapless wedding gown. "He has to lick it before it sticks it."

Rocio and Tiana helped Erin straightened out her gown. "And I'm assuming he can stick it pretty well. You seem a whole lot more relaxed and at peace," Rocio mentioned.

"Kieran is a great stress relief," Tiana couldn't help the smile on her face now. "The best damn stress relief I've ever had."

"Girl, get it while you can. In fact, get it for me while you're at it." Erin mentioned. "Get it all the time, please!"

"I do need some advice, though," Tiana began, "he wants me on top but I don't know how to…how to…"

"Ride the disco stick?" Rocio added.

"Play helicopter?" Erin teased.

"Being at the rodeo? Yee-haw!" Rocio laughed.

"Riding the stallion?" Erin laughed also.

"Oh my God, both of y'all..." Tiana pointed back and forth. "both of y'all..."

"You mean to tell me you never got on top with Cris?" Rocio asked.

"I never felt comfortable enough to do it," Tiana told a half-truth. The real truth was Christopher would make a comment about her appearance or weight. A few times he made a comment about how she didn't know how to have sex. She decided to forgo having sex with her husband all together. *I pushed him to cheat on me.* She relieved her mind and went back to the topic at hand. "I just need some advice because Kieran is insistent that I get on top."

"You need to relax. It's all mental, baby. You just need to concentrate on getting off and have him enjoy the ride," Erin suggested. "He'll guide you and tell you how to do it."

"Bend over a little when you're on top so your body is pressed against his. It's so fucking hot," Rocio fanned herself, "you'll be wishing you got on top sooner. You'll be able to hit the G-spot easier and quicker."

"And if all else fails, watch porno," Erin suggested, "in fact, I can recommend some good sites to you." Rocio and Tiana turned to face her, "oh, don't act like y'all are surprised by what I just said."

"Porn, huh?" Tiana bit her nail and twisted her mouth. "Hmm...I think that could work."

"I can recommend some good titles," Erin continued, "Um, there's Pussy Sales. Kinda corny but good. There's also Titty-Titty Bang Bang. Lick These Balls is pretty good…"

"I get your point, Erin," Tiana cut off her best friend. "Thank you for your suggestions."

****

"Is this little Tyson?" Zoe walked over to Kieran and greeted the little boy in his arms.

"It sure is," Kieran smiled. He stopped by his office to handle some business things before taking Tyson out for some new clothes. He was growing so fast. "He's hanging out with me while I'll take care of some things here." He made his way to his office. "How are things here?"

"Much more relaxed now that you're not here," Zoe kidded. "But seriously, no problems here. Everything's been running pretty smoothly."

"That's great to hear." Kieran placed Tyson on his desk. "Very good to hear."

"So how's the assignment? You've been there for a while now." Zoe mentioned.

"It's been a great assignment. Tiana is a great woman and well, little Tyson here is just a joy." Kieran smiled. "I really lucked out."

"I bet you did," Zoe folded her arms and leaned against the door. She noticed Kieran's demeanor. He had always been pretty laid-back but he was even more so upon being in the office. He couldn't stop smiling and fully doted on Tyson. "You're in love with her."

Kieran looked up at her. "What?"

"You're in love with her," Zoe repeated. "Yeah, he may be a joy and she may be a great woman but there's more to it. You love her."

"I never get involved with a client," Kieran stated. "It's against my personal beliefs."

"Well, you need to toss your personal beliefs out the window for a change," Zoe commented. "It's okay to fall in love, Kieran. It's okay to have someone love you back."

"Shouldn't you be serving the kids some snacks about now?" He asked.

"I'm going, I'm going," Zoe nodded, "I'm just saying, Kieran…fall in love and fall hard." She then left his office.

Kieran smiled at Tyson, who smiled back at him. "I already have."

NINE

It was moments like that Tiana regretted some of her past decisions.

She always bought name-brand and top quality products. She would rather invest five hundred dollars in a Kitchen-Aid mixer, knowing it will last for years than to spend a couple of hundred dollars on a knock-off. Her kitchen had the best of the best, as well did the rest of her home.

But with all of the cute toys she brought, she never took the time to learn how to operate the ones in the kitchen. She and Christopher ate out all the time. When that was getting pricey and old, the goal was to hire a chef to work the kitchen so she didn't have to. Now she was alone with a nanny and fancy machinery she didn't know how to use. Once she threw out the boxes, she hid the directions away somewhere.

She was so grateful for Kieran in more ways than one. "Okay, so I don't know how to do this," Tiana began.

Kieran stopped chopping vegetables and walked over to Tiana, who was standing in front of the pasta machine. The pair decided to have a nice quiet dinner at home, with just the three of them. "Why did you buy this if you don't know how to operate it?"

"I didn't buy it. I put it on the wedding registry because I thought it looked cool." Tiana shrugged. "I never planned to use it."

"You were going to hire a chef instead?" Kieran plugged in the machine and lightly dusted it off.

"I was getting around to it. It was on my to-do list before everything happened," she replied, "so it was going to be in use, just not by me."

"Well, it's easy," Kieran stood behind Tiana and grabbed some pasta. He carefully put it through the machine and spoke softly in her ear. "You just have to be careful with it and make sure it doesn't break."

Tiana softly bit her lip and fell back into Kieran's chest, his body comforting hers. Ooh, how she loved hearing Kieran's low rumble in her ear. Goosebumps formed along her arms and the heat slowly rose from her thighs to the pit of her stomach. It was bad enough he could do it without saying anything remotely sexual. "And what if it breaks?"

Kieran lightly caressed Tiana's arms. "Then you have to try again," he nibbled her earlobe, "that's all."

"We're not going to make dinner, baby," Tiana began to squirm, "we're not going to make dinner if we keep it up."

Kieran pressed Tiana's body against his. His cock was already hard and twitched a little in his jeans. "You know how to keep it up, *bella*," he moaned.

"Kieran…" Tiana moaned. Just when she was about to say 'eff it' to dinner and give a 'hell yes' to another round of oral in the kitchen, she heard Tyson's cry. "Saved by the baby…"

Kieran stepped away from Tiana. "For now."

Tiana looked back at Kieran. "We will continue later," she smiled before she left.

Kieran put more pasta through the machine. "Oh, you damn right we will…"

The pair fixed dinner and conversed on a variety of topics. Tiana shared some financial tips with Kieran to grow his business while he showed her some parenting tricks he had picked up along the years. After dinner, they had gelato while they watched the sky from Tiana's bedroom balcony.

"What are your dreams?" Tiana took a bite of her gelato.

"My dreams?" Kieran repeated.

"Yeah. You know more about my life story and what I want out of this life," she countered, "but I don't know yours."

Kieran took a bite of his gelato and contemplated his thoughts. He wondered if it was appropriate to tell her that he was in love with her. What he really wanted was to fulfill her wish and fill up her home with lots of babies. She had been married before and so had he, so he wasn't sure if marriage was in the cards for them both. But he did want forever with her.

"I have everything I want right here," Kieran grabbed Tiana's hand and kissed it. It wasn't a lie but it wasn't the entire truth. He would have to wait until it was the right moment.

"Besides that," Tiana rubbed his hand with her thumb, "I'm sure you have some desires?"

Kieran was stuck. He decided to chance it and let Tiana know what was in his heart. The worst she could do was reject him. "I would love to have kids one day."

"How many?"

"I don't know," Kieran shrugged, "I guess a few. I came from a big family so I'll be happy with three or four."

"Three or four kids sounds pretty big," Tiana added, "that's not a small number."

"When you have four other brothers, *anything* is smaller than that," he replied and Tiana smiled, "how many do you want?"

"I don't know," Tiana took another bite of gelato. "In addition to Tyson, I would like to have at least two more." What Tiana wanted to say was she wanted to have two more children—with Kieran. She kept her feelings silent, afraid of scaring him away after they'd had such a wonderful night.

There was an awkward silence between the pair. Neither knew what to say next, but they didn't want to fill the air with mindless chatter after a heavy topic. They finished their gelatos in silence and Kieran grabbed the bowls. He left for the kitchen when Tiana stopped him. "Yes?" He asked.

A sensual air passed between them and Tiana took the bowls away from Kieran and set them down. "I want you to teach me how to ride," she whispered.

Kieran shifted his weight and grabbed Tiana's hand. He caressed it as he looked into her brown orbs. "Ride what?"

Tiana's tongue darted her lips to moisten them. She felt the heat rising in her body and a yearning formed between her thighs. She wanted him—all night, all the time, and forever.

Kieran stepped closer to Tiana and kissed her neck, placing soft and sensual kisses along the way, causing a soft murmur to escape Tiana's lips. His hands played with her hard nipples through the shirt, before wandering over her body. "Tell me what you need, Tiana," his low baritone tickled her ear.

Tiana closed her eyes as Kieran continued to kiss her neck. She was in another place and another time. What she was feeling was stronger than real life. It seemed the earth stopped moving and it was just them alone in the world. "I want you to show me how to ride your dick," she whispered.

He pulled her tank top over her head and took his off as well. Tiana took stock at how ripped Kieran was, caressing his pecs and abs with her fingertips. She swallowed again, hard, and let out another breath. She needed to be with him and it was making her ache that they hadn't started yet.

Kieran locked eyes with Tiana and unbuttoned her shorts. He slowly pulled down the zipper and put his hands on her hips. He pulled her shorts down along with her panties and had Tiana step out of them. He took off his jeans and underwear and tossed them aside. His cock already jutted out and was rock hard, anxious to slip inside her.

He climbed on the bed, pulling Tiana down with him. His kisses were hot and hungry. He wanted this woman, *his* woman. He felt Tiana's heat and how wet she was. He moved her body on top of him and with a swift movement, he was inside her.

Tiana gasped and captured Kieran's lips again. "Shh…" He guided her. "I'm not going to let anything happen to you. Just follow my lead." He began to thrust upwards into her.

Tiana cradled Kieran and moaned in his neck. She was so tight around him and his cock…his cock was so thick, so big. It fit inside her so perfectly. She was a little more confident and sat up, taking all of Kieran inside her.

He interlocked his hands with hers and intently watched her move back and forth in a slow, rocking motion. Kieran saw her whole body, her facial expressions, her everything. She threw her head back and softly moaned as she opened more to him. She felt free.

It wasn't sex. It wasn't fucking. They were making love. They were joined together as their bodies danced and collided with each other, finding a nice rhythm between them.

"That's it, baby," he encouraged her, "ride me. Don't worry about anything else right now."

Tiana leaned over and began to rock her body against Kieran's. She increased her rhythm as her breasts were pressed up against his chest, his hands sliding up and down her ass, and her pussy tightly clenching his cock. She wanted more and demanded more. "Oh fuck, Kieran…" she moaned.

"You like that cock, *bella*?" Kieran moaned in her ear. His jagged breathing matched hers. "You like riding my big cock?"

"Oh shit, Kieran…" His words made Tiana ride him faster. The moans coming out were deep and guttural, from the pit of her stomach. She was close, so close to her orgasm.

"You want to cum, *bella*? You want to cum over my dick?" He encouraged.

Tiana's legs began to shake and she rode faster. The first coils of her orgasm were approaching. Her toes curled, her pussy began to contract, and sweat coated her body. "Kieran…Kieran…"

"Cum, *bella*…let go," he encouraged.

Tiana fisted the sheets and let out a loud cry, screaming several expletives. She'd never felt so free, so raw, as when she made love to him. She let go of her inhibitions and worries. When she finally came down from her high, Tiana looked down at her boyfriend, who was smiling big at her. "I think I woke up Tyson."

"I'll go check on him," Kieran eased Tiana off him. He kissed her softly. "I'll be right back." He left for the nursery.

Tiana lay back down in bed and looked up at the ceiling. She was going have to be able to control her moans more in bed with

Kieran. Tyson may have slept through what he heard but he was still an infant. It would be a different ball game when he got older.

"He's fine. Slept right through everything," Kieran climbed back in bed with Tiana.

"I need to learn how to be quiet," Tiana snuggled with her boyfriend. "I can't be that vocal."

"You'll figure out a way," Kieran kissed her forehead.

"But how?" Tiana wondered.

Kieran was waiting for her to say something. It was his cue to act. "Lay down on your stomach," he ordered.

Tiana turned around and did what Kieran requested. "What are you…"

"Don't talk," he instructed. He grabbed a pillow and lifted it under Tiana's pelvis. He stroked his cock again until it was hard. He then spread her ass cheeks and entered inside her pussy. He laid on top of her. "Bite the pillow when it becomes too much," he whispered.

He began to move inside her, his balls pressing against her ass cheeks. He reached up and grabbed Tiana's wrists, holding them to steady himself. "Fuck, Tiana…" he breathed. "Fuck, *bella*…"

Tiana panted and fisted the sheets again. The new position increased the pressure and friction between them and Kieran completely filled Tiana. He moved inside her slowly, stretching her as she once again accommodated his cock. He quickened his thrusts, his balls slapping against her ass.

He let go of her wrists and steadied himself on his hands and moved inside her. He kissed the sweat off her back as he listened to her muffled moans and cries, calling his name, begging the high heavens, finally letting go of everything in her life.

Tiana's legs began to shake and she gripped tighter around his cock. "Kieran, baby…" she moaned.

"Bite the pillow," he encouraged as he thrust relentlessly into her, "I want to fuck your ass tonight. You want to give me your ass, don't you, baby?"

Tiana had only tried anal a handful of times in her past and it was an experience she didn't particularly want to write home about. But at that moment, she wanted Kieran to test her body. "Yes, baby," Tiana breathed.

"Tell me, Tiana…tell me what you want from me," Kieran continued to thrust inside her.

The more Kieran taunted her, the more Tiana wanted him. "Fuck my ass," she begged him.

Kieran pulled out of Tiana and turned her on her side. He lifted one leg up and slowly pushed into her. Tiana gasped and licked her lips at the new friction. He filled her completely and she wasn't sure she could take all of him. Kieran showered her neck with soft kisses while a free hand explored her body. "Tell me when you're ready, baby," he whispered.

"I am," Tiana nodded.

Kieran pushed more into Tiana, sliding in and out of her. He reached over and played with her pearl as he glided in and out of her. They were entwined together, his hands once again exploring her body, softly pinching her nipples and grabbing at her waist. Tiana bit and moaned into another pillow, begging Kieran to continue and not stop pleasing her.

He furiously rubbed her clit as he pushed more into her. "Are you going to cum for me, *bella*? Are you going to cum?" He begged her.

"Fuck, Kieran…"Tiana's body convulsed as she came, floating on a cloud and into another world. The orgasm was intense and her whole body shook. She bit the pillow hard and again fisted the sheets.

Kieran soon came after her, spilling himself into her. "Damn, Tiana," his low voice kissed her ear, "damn, baby, you're incredible."

****

"What color is this?" Kieran looked at the nail polish bottle.

"That is Sinful Delight," Tiana smiled.

"Sinful Delight, huh?" Kieran took out the nail polish brush and began to paint his girlfriend's toenails. "You naughty girl."

After the last lovemaking round, the couple engaged in pillow talk on a variety of topics. The discussion led to Tiana giving some Kieran some financial tips and she shared how she gives herself her own manicures and pedicures. "I can be," Tiana admired the sight before her. A man painting her toenails. No, *her* man painting her toenails. That feeling was orgasmic.

Kieran painted one foot and moved on to the other. After Tiana gave herself a foot soak, she also soaked Kieran's feet and gave him a pedicure, which he thought was out of this world. He quickly started planning to get regular pedicures in the future. "What are you afraid of?"

Tiana was shot back down to earth with Kieran's question. "That's a heavy topic after sex."

"I'm trying to get to know my girlfriend." Kieran clarified. "Is that a crime?"

Tiana naturally assumed she was Kieran's girlfriend but it was nice to hear him actually say it. "I'm your girlfriend, now?"

"Are you not?" He countered.

Kieran called her bluff. It was match point. "I guess I am."

"You don't have to be if you don't want to be," Kieran blew a little on her toes. "I'm certainly not forcing you."

Tiana re-focused her attention on Kieran. There was something so sensual about seeing a man take care of his woman's feet. "No, it's not that."

"Then what is it?" He asked.

"I'm not about that life if that's what you're expecting." Tiana replied.

Kieran was quiet as he did a quick glance over at Tiana's nails. "I thought we went over this last night?" He asked.

"You're not going to be my boy toy," Tiana stated.

Kieran blew on Tiana's nails. "Oh, you don't want to play with me in bed?"

"You know what I mean," Tiana shyly licked her lips. "I'm not about that life."

"What life are you talking about?" He asked.

"My son comes first. I'm not about fancy trips around the world. Expensive shopping sprees. Dinner parties with celebrities and other famous people. I only deal with celebrities because I have to, not because I want to. I'm very frugal with my money and occasionally splurge," she explained, "but I don't want you to think I'm some ready-made ATM at your disposal."

Kieran slowly nodded as he focused on Tiana's toenails. "Do you do this to all of your boyfriends?"

Tiana's eyes narrowed in on her boyfriend. "Do what?"

Kieran painted another coat of polish on Tiana's nails. "The scare tactic."

Was she trying to scare him? She didn't think so. *Politely warning* him sounded better in her head. "I never had a man get so profound with me and want to get to know me."

Kieran should've been surprised but he wasn't. Tiana didn't reveal too much about her marriage but it was pretty clear that Christopher didn't care about her one way or another. Kieran wanted to ask Tiana why she stayed in her marriage as long as she did but he already knew the answer. *Keeping up appearances.* "I want to know whatever I can about you," Kieran placed the brush back inside the polish bottle. He gently blew on Tiana's toes. "You're not obligated to tell me anything."

"Alone," she blurted.

Kieran stopped blowing on Tiana's toes. Was she kicking him out of her house? Maybe he crossed a line he shouldn't have. "I'm sorry, Tiana, I really didn't…"

"I'm afraid of being alone," she clarified, "I'm afraid I'm not going to have someone to grow old with."

There was a long silence between the pair. Now Tiana felt she was the one that crossed a line. When she was about to make some cheesy joke to break the silence, Kieran interrupted her. "You'll never be alone as long as I'm around."

"You're making promises you can't possibly keep, Kieran," she replied.

"You say that as if you know what I'm all about," Kieran nodded and began painting Tiana's nails again.

Tiana felt she dug herself deeper and deeper into a hole. Every time she opened her mouth, something stupid came out of it. "Forget I said anything," she mumbled.

"Come with me to Staten Island," Kieran softly spoke.

"What? Staten Island?"

"I'm giving you an opportunity to see me in my hometown with my friends and family," he added, "you can decide after you've met everyone and seen me in my element, if you still want to take a chance on me."

"You drive a hard bargain, Kieran," Tiana admitted. The offer was too good to refuse. "I need to find a sitter for Tyson."

"Bring him with us," Kieran shrugged.

"You want me to bring a teething baby with us on a plane?" She questioned.

"You have the gel and chew toys for him," Kieran suggested. "I don't see why it would be a problem."

"We probably won't find a hotel so late."

"We'll stay at my mom's. She's anxious to meet you and Tyson."

Tiana had to do a double-take. Did she really hear what she just heard? "You told your mother about me?"

"I tell my mother everything," Kieran began massaging Tiana's foot.

Tiana's eyes rolled in the back of her head. Kieran's hands were orgasmic. "And what did you tell your mother exactly?"

"I told her that I met this magnificent woman who has a son and I'm falling in love with her," Kieran said matter-of-factly. "Was there something else I should've said instead?"

Tiana wanted to respond with an 'I love you'. She wanted to shout it from the rooftops. She wanted to dance and sing. The man she wanted to be with just committed to her. He told his mother about her. They were living together. It was the beginning of a beautiful relationship!

Instead she took the cautious route. She loved Kieran but she was still recovering from her broken marriage. "I feel the same way, too."

TEN

"I'll be on vacation for a week, visiting my family on Staten Island," Kieran instructed his staff at the weekly meeting. "If anything urgent comes up, you know how to reach me. I'm always available. Does anyone have any questions?"

"I do," Zoe raised a hand.

"Besides Zoe," Kieran grinned.

"Hey! Hey! I might have a legitimate question, now." Zoe feigned hurt feelings.

"Okay, Zoe. What is your question?"

"Are you going to come back married?" She smiled.

"And that concludes this meeting," Kieran dismissed everyone. "I'll see everyone in about two weeks." He began to put away papers as everyone left.

Zoe stayed behind and waited until it was just her and Kieran in the room. "So you're bringing her to meet the mother? Sounds serious."

Kieran knew he shouldn't entertain his nosy assistant even if he was curious how she found out. "How did you know that?"

"Oh, I don't know," Zoe mischievously grinned. "I just happened to be watching the *Today* show and saw a financial analyst by the name of Tiana Morris giving out financial tips when one is traveling and she mentioned how she was going to visit Staten Island for the first time and what do you know? You're from there!"

"Why did I hire you again?" Kieran asked.

"Because I'm the only woman who can tolerate you," Zoe smiled. "Have a safe trip. Bring back me back something!" She left the conference room.

Kieran picked up Tyson from the floor. The last several weeks with Tiana had been nothing short of amazing. Sure, he could chalk it up to new and exciting love. But there was something different about her. There was something magical about this time around. It wasn't just sex; Kieran had been in lust more than he had been in love. It wasn't just a new woman; Tiana was above and beyond any woman he'd ever dated.

He could finally admit he was in love with her. Head over heels, sappy songs on the radio, everything-is-coming-up-roses in love with her. With little Tyson in the mix, the little boy just completed the one thing Kieran had always wanted—a family of his own. "Are you ready, little man? You're going to meet my family. If things go well, you're going to meet your new *nonna*."

****

"Okay, your flight is booked!" Allison handed Tiana her travel packet. "Here is your flight information, all checked-in. Why didn't you take a private plane? It would be easier on all three of you."

"I thought about it," Tiana sincerely wished she had booked a private plane. She always hated hearing a screaming baby when she traveled and she feared Tyson was going to become the one thing she couldn't stand. "But I didn't want Kieran to think I was all about being fancy by getting a private plane."

"Yeah, because those first-class tickets you purchased told otherwise," Allison folded her arms and smiled.

"You know what I mean," Tiana leaned back in her chair. "I still don't know if he's with me for me or my lifestyle."

"Well, I have something for you," Allison disappeared and reappeared a short while later, "here's some clear-cut evidence he's not with you for the money."

Tiana stared down at the information before her. She couldn't believe what she was seeing. In front of her was a picture of Kieran, his brothers, and their mother holding a very big check with an equally big dollar amount. "Where did you get this?"

"Google is your friend."

****

Kieran and Tiana boarded their plane and got settled with Tyson, who was peacefully sleeping. Tiana cherished that time. She knew it was only a matter of hours before her son would be wide awake and wailing to his heart's content.

"So tell me about your family?" She asked as she buckled up. "Tell me some more about your brothers."

"The craziest fools you'll ever meet," Kieran laughed, "but I love them to death. Couldn't ask for better brothers. Nicolas is the oldest. He's an English professor at NYU and studying to get his Master's degree. He's very popular with his female students, though; I told him he needs to quit that before the school has a lawsuit on their hands.

"Joey is the middle son and he and our second-youngest brother, Eli, help run my mom's floral business. Joey is looking for Ms. Right Now while Eli just got married a few years ago and finally made our mother into a *nonna* of her own. They have the flagship store in Manhattan and just opened up another one in New York City. They hope to expand soon to Long Island."

"Finally, there's Antonio, the playboy. He still lives at home and is a barber. He says he stays at home to watch over our mother but I think he just doesn't want to move out quite yet. Mom still does his laundry." Kieran shook his head, "there's always one in the family."

"Oh, come on, four out of five aren't bad," Tiana replied.

Kieran gave Tiana a disbelieving look. "Wait until you meet Tony."

Tiana was quiet for a brief moment until she found the courage to talk to Kieran about what she learned that morning. She began to wonder if there was more to Kieran than she realized. "Why didn't you tell me you won the lottery?" She asked.

Kieran got settled into his seat and let it back a little. He wondered how long it was going to take Tiana to find that information out about him. "I didn't," he replied, "my mother did."

"But your mother is wealthy," Tiana added.

"Correction: my mother is rich," Kieran replied, stating the difference between the two, "*you're* wealthy."

"Still," Tiana pressed, "you have money."

Kieran was quiet for a moment before he spoke again. "Imagine growing up and seeing your mother come home from working at a diner. She's exhausted and been on her feet for most of the day already, tending to needy customers, handling heavy trays, and getting the right orders. She only can rest for an hour or two before she gets back up and works her other job doing janitorial work. And when she leaves that job, she can only sleep for a few hours before she gets up and does the whole thing all over again. And she does that day in and day out for *years*. She works weekends if she needs to. If I wanted that new stereo, she'd put in an extra shift to make sure I got it. If my brother wanted that new bike every other kid has, she'd put it a few more shifts to make sure he got it. We never had a lot of money growing up, but never went without. She made sure the lights were on, the gas was on, and there was food in the fridge. Most importantly, she made sure there was a roof over our heads. And she taught us the value of a dollar.

"Now imagine that your mother—the same one who's been busting her ass for as long as you can remember—decided one day she's going to play the lottery for fun, not thinking she's going to win anything. But she wins and she wins big. She doesn't have to work anymore. She can fly to those countries she's always wanted to visit. She can afford new and better quality clothing instead of re-sewing the torn and tattered ones she's had for years. She can finally afford a nice pair of comfortable shoes—several of them, actually. She can finally afford to fix those holes in the walls and that leaking faucet that's been driving up her water bill. And that same, unselfish mother," Kieran's voice cracked a little and he paused before he was overcome with emotion. "That same, unselfish mother who took you in when you felt the world was against you and your luck had run out, gives you some money so you can go to school and start your own business. So yes, Tiana, my mother is rich but I am not."

Tiana grabbed Kieran's hand and squeezed it. He was her much-needed reality check. "Your mother is a great woman."

"My mother has always been my biggest cheerleader," Kieran squeezed Tiana's hand back, "and now I have another one."

****

Nicola D'Amato took out her homemade lasagna. A proud smile formed on her face once the aromas of basil, cheese, and tomato sauce tickled her nose. After her lottery win some ten years earlier, she quit her jobs to start the floral business, Madre's, which she operated with her sons, Joey and Eli. She took pride in her flowers and was sought-after by celebrities, socialites, and event planners for their weddings and private parties. She also managed a non-profit for low-income women to acquire job skills and other classes for the workforce. She was recently named one of most influential people in New York.

She was of average height with ebony hair and sharp, hazel eyes that always told her sons what she really thought about them without ever having to say a word. "Perfect," Nicola smiled at her lasagna. "Absolutely perfect!"

"Hey mom, when is Kieran coming in?" The oldest, Nicolas, commented to his mother. He didn't look like a college professor and certainly didn't act like one, either. He would constantly bring up pop culture references when instructing his students about Shakespeare to get them to understand what he was teaching them. He had a muscular build he kept hidden under sweater vests and slacks. He had his dark hair neatly trimmed and wore black hipster frames.

"Anytime now! He and Tiana should be arriving soon." Nicola grabbed fresh pepper and sprinkled a little on the salad. She then approached her youngest son. "Tony, make sure the rooms are cleaned and there's plenty of towels in the bathrooms. They'll be staying here."

"All right, mom," Tony then left the living room.

"Kieran's bringing home Ms. Fancy Pants," The middle son, Joey, snickered as he set the table. He was built just like his older brother and visited the gym on a daily basis. He drove an Escalade and entertained several girlfriends all over New York. "You never act like this with my girlfriends."

"Well, if you didn't bring home those tramps, I would give them the same treatment," Nicola sneered.

"Owned!" Eli laughed as put out the food on the table.

"What's funny, punk?" Joey commented. "Hey, at least I ain't no lady-whipped punk like you are."

"Oh, yes," Eli nodded. He was tall with muscular tawny skin that seemed to be kissed by the sun. He had intense hazel eyes and never met a stranger he didn't like. He had been happily married to his high-school sweetheart, Faith, for three years. "Because I have a woman who will get on her knees and service me whenever I want while you have to go out and beg for it, I'm a punk? Gotcha."

"Madre, did you hear what he said about your innocent daughter-in-law?" Joey commented.

"Oh, you two are giving me a headache already!" Nicola yelled.

****

"Well, here we are," Kieran stepped out of the cab with Tyson in the car seat. He looked up at the renovated house his mother lived in. When he was growing up, it was just two bedrooms and two bathrooms for all six of them. Now there were two additional bedrooms, a bathroom, and an added den. It was plenty of room for everyone and their families. *We have come a long way.*

Tiana stepped out of the cab and bundled up. New York in the fall was quite different from Southern California. In LA, she could still go out to work wearing a tank top. In Staten Island, she felt her teeth clack. It was something she would have to get used to. "So this is it, huh?" Tiana looked at the home. "It's a lovely home."

"Now it is," Kieran handed Tyson to Tiana while he gathered their belongings. "It wasn't always like this."

Suddenly, a small biracial child shot out from the door and ran to Kieran. "Crayon! Crayon!" The little boy jumped up and down. "Daddy, Crayon is here!"

A big smile grew on Tiana's face. "Crayon?"

"He's still trying to pronounce Kieran. He almost got it," he smiled back at her.

Eli walked out and gave his older brother a big hug. "Kieran! Man, it's so good to see you!" Eli kissed both Kieran's cheeks. "It's about time you show your face around here again. You need to start coming home more often."

"I come home every six months," Kieran offered.

"Yeah, well, you need to do it every three. You know how mom gets," Eli turned his attention to Tiana and Tyson. "And you must be the beautiful woman who has given my brother a life again. Pleasure to meet you, Tiana, and hello to you, little Tyson." He waved at him. "I'm Eli and this is my son, Nathan. Come on in before you catch a cold out here. I know how you Cali women are."

Eli took the car seat away from Tiana and went into the house with Nathan. Tiana pulled Kieran aside before they went in. "You didn't tell me you had a biracial nephew?" She was pleasantly surprised.

"I didn't think there was anything to tell," Kieran raised an eyebrow, "we're not in the 1950s."

"I just didn't think your family would be so open to me being here," she replied.

"We weren't raised like that," Kieran's voice was serious. "And most people in this neighborhood don't care about that stuff."

"I didn't think you were. It's just…it's just…honestly, I don't even know anymore." Tiana said, exasperated. "Ever since I met you, it seems everything I ever known has been thrown out the window."

Kieran captured Tiana's lips with his in a searing kiss. "Good. I hope it stays that way."

"Hey! Do you want to come in sometime for some food or should I get out the tent for you?" Tony called from inside the house.

****

Tiana's head was stuck in a game of tennis as she watched all the food pass back and forth at the table. A hearty helping of lasagna, fried eggplant, and plenty of bread and salad was passed throughout the large family table, big enough to hold ten people. Kieran fixed her plate, making sure she had plenty of food on it and Tiana wondered how she was going to be able to clean it off. Her stomach wasn't *that* big.

She took stock of Kieran's brothers. They were all attractive and easy on the eyes. They were all around the same height—some shorter or taller—and had muscular builds. Tiana thought about Nicola's grocery bill when the boys were younger. It must've been through the roof.

"It's okay to be intimidated at first," Faith quietly said to Tiana as she sat next to her. She was a short Black female with natural light brown curls and a curvy body. She had a warm demeanor and a soft voice. "The first dinner is always the worst but after the second one, you'll wonder why you were ever nervous to begin with."

"It's so much…" Tiana looked around and then back at the heaping portion on her plate. "I'm never going to be able to finish this."

"Don't worry about it," Faith passed the breadsticks. "They will finish it for you if you can't. Food doesn't get wasted at this house."

"Everyone, everyone!" Nicola finally sat down at the head chair. "Let's grab hands and say grace. Time to give thanks."

After everyone said grace, they all begin eating. "So, Tiana," Tony took a bite of his lasagna, "do you have any other rich friends like yourself?"

Eli kicked his brother underneath the table and Tony howled. "Hey, what was that for?" Tony yelled.

"*Chiudi il becco*!" Eli snickered.

"Why in the hell you asking her about her private business like that?" Joey commented.

"What are you doing, man?" Nicolas asked Tony. "You act like you were raised by a pack of wolves."

"No, I just grew up with them," Tony rubbed his shin.

"It's okay," Tiana smiled at the men defending her honor. Kieran's brothers reminded her of her guy friends. "All of my girlfriends are taken."

"Except one," Kieran mentioned.

Tiana knew Kieran was talking about Denise. "I'm not subjecting your brother to that," she replied.

"It's okay, Tiana," Joey chimed in, "I'll take her."

"Fool, you'll take a blow-up doll if it could walk," Tony replied.

"No, that's your last girlfriend," Joey replied.

Faith looked over at Nicola. "How did you manage this for so long?"

"Easy," Nicola tore off a piece of a breadstick and popped it in her mouth. "I was never here."

****

After dinner and good-byes, Tiana walked upstairs and got Tyson ready for bed. She gave him a bath and changed him into his pajamas when Nicola appeared at her doorway. "May I come in?" She asked.

"Sure, Nicola," Tiana smiled. "I was getting little man ready for bed. He's had a long day."

Nicola sat on the bed and smiled down at Tyson, who smiled back at her. "How old is he now?"

"Nine months," Tiana was amazed at the thought. It seemed time was slipping away from her.

"And before you know it, he'll be in kindergarten, then high school, and then you'll be watching him at his first dance at his wedding..." Nicola reminisced. "Enjoy the quiet moments as much as you can."

Tiana smiled warmly at her son. "Tell me about it!"

"So about you and Kieran," Nicola began, "how serious are you two?"

Tiana shrugged. "We just started dating not too long ago so we're taking it slow."

"You're taking it slow?" Nicola asked. "But he's been living with you for the past three months?"

"He has his own house he stays in…"

"And he watches over your son…"

"Well, I pay him to do so…"

"He has his own money so he's not after yours…"

"Well, I never thought he wanted me for my money…"

"And he's been teaching you how to cook. Plus, I know that smile on your face," Nicola mentioned, "only a woman in love has that smile."

Tiana finished dressing Tyson and Nicola picked him up. "I'm in the middle of going through a divorce, Nicola. I can't promise anything to Kieran, at least not yet."

"I understand that and so does he," Nicola softly bounced Tyson on her hip.

A short silence stood between the pair before Tiana spoke again. "So why do I have the feeling that you don't believe me?"

"It's not that I don't believe you, Tiana. I know you're a good woman. I always follow your financial advice and read your articles," Nicola replied to which Tiana gave a half-grin. "I'm a fan of yours. But I'm also a bigger fan of my son. He'll wait as long as he needs to but he won't wait around forever. If you're not sure about how you want to proceed with your relationship, you need to let him know as soon as possible so he can find someone who is more suitable for him. It's only fair to all three of you."

Tiana lightly sighed. Maybe she was dragging her feet admitting her feelings. Kieran declared his love for her and she was still acting like a child who's unsure about which toy she wanted to play with first. "Thank you."

"Not a problem," Nicola smiled, "I'll take little Tyson with me tonight so you two can have some privacy and be alone. I have a bassinet in my room so he'll be safe. *"Buona notte e sogni d'oro, Tiana."* She walked out of the room.

"Buona notte, Nicola," Tiana replied. She grabbed some clothing and headed to the bathroom for a nice, hot shower. She closed her eyes as she felt the hot water beat on her skin. Nicola was right. Rocio and Erin were right. Tiana needed to just admit to Kieran her feelings towards him. It was clear he felt the same way. She couldn't see anyone else other than Kieran in her life and the way he cared about Tyson…he showed more love for the little boy in just a few months than Christopher ever did and still hasn't. *What am I doing?*

Tiana got out of the shower and dried off. She quickly changed into her pajamas and went to bed. She was going to tell Kieran how much she was in love with him and then show him. There was no way that man was going to slip through her fingers.

ELEVEN

Kieran sat around at the card table with his brothers, sipping on his beer and looking at his poker cards. Growing up they never had much money so they would always wager clothing, shoes, or video games. When things were really lean, they would wager who would do chores.

As they grew older, whenever Kieran and his brothers got together for cards, they would still wager chores and insignificant items like a bouquet of flowers from the shop, a couple of tutoring sessions from Nicolas, a week of child care from Kieran's business, or a haircut for a couple of months from Tony's barber shop. The men knew how it was to be without money and never dared to wager a dime of it, despite all of them having their own.

"So how much longer do you plan on working for Tiana now that you're a couple?" Eli asked as he looked at his cards.

"I don't know," Kieran folded his cards and sipped his beer. "I guess whenever she feels comfortable enough."

"That's the life, man," Tony stroked his goatee, "being with a rich woman, living in her mansion, and all you have to do is watch her kid and give her the salami every so often."

Nicolas studied his cards. "Can someone please…?"

Eli reached over and slapped the back of Tony's head. "Thank you," Joey shook his head.

"Hey!" Tony rubbed his head. "What did I say?"

"She's a great woman, Kieran," Nicolas picked up his cards again. "You picked a winner this time."

"Better than the last one," Joey sipped his beer.

"Oh much better than the last one," Eli agreed, "I'm in."

"What's your wager?" Tony asked.

"A dozen roses," Eli replied.

"Long-stemmed?" Joey asked.

Eli looked back at his cards. "Yeah, let's go for long-stemmed. I'm confident."

"Speaking of the last one," Tony spoke to Kieran, "wanna know what your lovely ex has been up to lately?"

"Not really," Kieran replied. His ex-wife, Jalara, still left a sour taste in his mouth.

"She's working at the Lovely Kitten," Tony replied, causing amused stares from his brothers, "or so I've heard."

Kieran knew he shouldn't entertain his brother but he was curious. "How long has she been working the pole?"

"I don't know. I'm in with two free haircuts," Tony placed his bet. "I heard it from one of my boys that's what she does. Apparently she's been asking about you."

"I bet she has," Kieran took another sip of beer, "Ten thousand dollars doesn't go very far."

"So what are your plans with Tiana?" Joey folded his cards. "Pretty serious for you to bring her and her kid along?"

"I don't know," Kieran let out a soft sigh, "she's in the process of going through a divorce and she admitted she's not trying to get involved with anyone."

"But she came with you?" Nicolas folded his cards. "I'm thinking what she said isn't matching up with what she's doing."

"I stopped trying to figure out women a long time ago," Kieran added, "every time I think I figured one out, I couldn't have been more wrong."

"Are you ready to walk away if she rejects you?" Eli asked.

"That's the million-dollar question," Kieran leaned back in his chair. "I'm going to have to if she does."

"What about her kid?" Tony asked. "What about him?"

"That's the problem of getting involved with women who have children," Kieran took another sip of beer, "even if things don't work out with the mom, you still want to see the child. But if things really don't work out with Tiana, I will have to walk away from Tyson as well, and that really sucks."

****

Hours later, Kieran went to bed. He saw Tiana was already sleeping so he walked over to his mother's room to check on her and Tyson before he headed back to his bedroom.

He was in the middle of getting undressed when Tiana opened her eyes. "I'm sorry, *bella*. I didn't mean to wake you."

"It's okay, baby," Tiana yawned, "you didn't disrupt me at all. Did you all have fun playing poker?"

"Yeah, Nick cleaned house," Kieran removed his socks and climbed into bed. "Two months of haircuts and four dozen roses. Lucky bastard."

Tiana smiled. "Well, maybe next time?"

"Nah, I was just playing for fun," Kieran snuggled up to his girlfriend. "I won the best prize already." He kissed her cheek.

Tiana felt that was her cue. "Kieran, baby, we need to talk."

Kieran immediately withdrew from her. He knew whenever a woman uttered those words; it was the kiss of death. He wondered which brother was the final nail in the coffin. It reminded him to have a talk with Tony. "I'm listening."

Tiana sat up in bed and turned the light on. She wanted to read his eyes. "You know I'm in the process of getting divorced and what's it done to my psyche. Cris was an awful husband and has been a terrible father to Tyson. And because of everything, I'm guarded. And I'm raw. I wasn't planning to date again for a very long time and I wasn't thinking about bringing anyone around Tyson until I knew there was a definite future." She paused and closed her eyes, trying to find the courage to continue. "Then I met you.

"You accept my faults, and love me anyway. You see my boring lifestyle, and love me anyway. My son can be so fussy and after dealing with him all day, every day, you love him anyway." Tiana held Kieran's hand. "I'm going to be guarded a little longer and I still have some trust issues to sort through. But if you can bear with me, I promise you won't regret it."

"Tiana, I'll wait for you," Kieran replied, "but only if you let me."

"I don't want you to wait," Tiana got out of bed. She removed her pajamas and hair wrap, letting her locks fall down. "Kieran, I love you. This is me—naked and raw—with no expensive gown, no fancy makeup, no reservations, telling you I love you."

Kieran got out of bed and removed his boxer briefs. "This is me, naked and raw, without the daycare, without the crazy brothers, without my rich family, telling you I love you." He climbed on the bed and Tiana met him halfway.

Tiana briefly closed her eyes when Kieran caressed her hard nipples. She lightly wet her lips in anticipation. "So, what do we do now?"

Kieran wrapped an arm around Tiana's waist and pulled her tight against his body. He was hard and his cock glistened with pre-cum. He kissed her lips before trailing his tongue down to her neck. "I guess we have to make it official, don't we?" He grabbed her face with both hands and kissed her.

His kisses were hot and wet and Tiana felt that yearning inside her. She wanted this man. She wanted *her* man. She didn't want to play the childish games anymore. She didn't want to have any more reservations. She loved him and wanted to be with him.

Her body became flushed as she felt Kieran's cock stir against her thigh. He forced his tongue inside and Tiana relished in the velvet roughness of it. Kieran's impatient hands wandered all over her body, cupping her ass and squeezing her breasts, wanting to feel, taste, and touch more.

They fell onto the bed and Kieran rolled on top of Tiana. He saw the hunger in her eyes, the need to love and be loved. With a quick movement, he entered her, filling her as she tightly accommodated him.

They rocked in unison as they surrendered their love to each other. Their mouths hungry for each other as Kieran relentlessly drove into Tiana, solidifying their union and their bond.

Tiana clutched at Kieran's back as she climaxed, her body quietly shuddering, and a small moan escaping her lips. He soon followed her and became still. He closed his eyes as he emptied in her, relieving himself of the frustration of not knowing where he stood and welcoming the opportunity to explore a new relationship with the woman he loved so much.

He reached down and captured her lips once again, rolling off Tiana in the process. As Tiana drifted off into a peaceful sleep, Kieran lay awake and thought about what just happened that night.

He was in way over his head. He just hoped he wasn't making a big mistake.

****

Kieran woke up to the familiar scent of his mother's biscuits. In the past, when she had a rare day off from both jobs, she'd always made a big breakfast for everyone. He eased himself out of the bed and slipped on some clothing. He quickly brushed his teeth and then joined his mother in the kitchen. "*Buongiorno*, mamma," he kissed her cheek.

"*Buongiorno*, *il figlio*. How did you and Tiana sleep last night?" She took out the orange juice.

Kieran walked over to the playpen Tyson was in and picked him up. It warmed Nicola's heart to see how in love he was with Tyson. "We slept just fine. I hope Tyson wasn't too much trouble?"

"Oh, he was just fine!" Nicola scrambled the eggs in a mixing bowl. "Gave me no problems at all!"

"That's great to hear," Kieran bounced Tyson a little, causing the infant to giggle. "I was a little concerned last night so I…"

"I dreamt of rainbows," Nicola smiled.

Kieran placed Tyson back in the playpen. He then headed to the dining room to begin setting up the table. He concentrated on the place setting and kept quiet.

"I thought that news would make you hopeful," Nicola continued to scramble the eggs.

Kieran shrugged. "I don't know what to say."

"Well, you know what happens each time I dream about rainbows," Nicola checked the sizzling bacon in the next pan.

"Someone gets pregnant," Kieran finished setting the table.

There was a long silence between the pair as Kieran finished setting the table and Nicola put the eggs and bacon on a platter. "*Può parlare più lentamente?* Please slow down with what you're saying, Kieran. I can't keep up."

"What makes you think it's going to be me and not the others?" He referenced to his brothers.

"Because I saw *your* face. And I saw *her* face," Nicola referred to Tiana. "I'm not wrong."

"That doesn't mean there's a baby in the future," Kieran hated dismissing his mother but felt the need to correct her.

Nicola smiled as she put the food on the table. "Funny how Eli and Faith said exactly the same thing."

Kieran helped his mother with the rest of the food. "It's too soon for that."

"Funny how *she* said the same thing last night," Nicola grinned as she spoke about Tiana.

His mother's admission caused Kieran to do a double-take. "You spoke to her about us?"

"Of course I did," Nicola set out the orange juice. "I wanted to make sure you both knew what you were getting into."

A slow grin formed on Kieran's face. He began to connect the dots. His mother had a breakthrough with Tiana he had thought was impossible. He gave his mother a big hug. "Thank you, mamma."

"You're welcome, *il figlio*," Nicola hugged back. "Just promise me one thing."

"Hmm?"

"I want to see my grandbaby. Either you come here or I'll go to California. I'm not into that Skype-thing that's all the rage."

"Good morning, everyone!" Tiana walked into the kitchen. "Wow, Nicola. Everything smells great!"

"Thank you so much, Tiana. Everyone will be here shortly," Nicola walked back into the kitchen. "Do you want coffee or tea?"

Tiana kissed her boyfriend and walked over to the playpen and picked up her son. "I'll have some coffee if you have some."

"Sounds good," Nicola took out a couple of mugs and poured some coffee. "Oh, *il figlio*, I forgot to mention I thought I heard a mouse last night."

"A mouse?" Kieran asked. "Where?"

"Down the hall," Nicola replied, "Tiana, do you take cream or sugar?"

"Both, Nicola," she replied, "thanks."

"The funny thing is I only heard it really late at night," Nicola poured some cream in her mug and a couple scoops of sugar, "sounded like some shuffling. I thought I heard a squeak."

Kieran's eyes widened and he looked over to Tiana, who had equally wide eyes. His mother heard them making love. "I'll check it after breakfast, mamma."

"Good," Nicola sipped her coffee, "and when you check for the mouse, can you let me know if you find a rainbow as well?"

****

"You know I don't have to go out tonight, *bella*," Kieran fixed himself up in the mirror, "I came here to show you around, not go out with my brothers. I see them all the time."

"You don't see them often," Tiana cuddled with Tyson on the bed. "Besides, Faith and Nathan are coming by and we're going to have some fun with your mother tonight. You need to go out and enjoy being with your brothers."

Kieran leaned over the bed and kissed Tiana, then Tyson. "I promise to be good," he spoke quietly.

"I know you will. Have fun, baby," Tiana waved him goodbye.

Kieran walked down the stairs and kissed his mother goodbye. "I'll be back later, mamma."

"See you later, *il figlio*," Nicola prepared the snacks for the evening.

Kieran's brothers soon joined him in the kitchen. "Are you ready to go, man?" Joey asked.

"Ready to go," Kieran replied. "Let's go."

The brothers loaded up in Joey's Escalade and headed out. "What's the plan for tonight?" Kieran asked.

"The Lovely Kitten," Joey navigated down the street.

"Jesus Christ," Kieran huffed, "for real?"

"Come on, man," Joey glanced at his brother through the rearview mirror, "aren't you curious?"

"Not really," Kieran looked out the window.

"We're just going to go in and see how she's doing and then leave," Tony spoke from the front passenger seat, "no harm, no foul."

"Why do I need to see her?" Kieran asked. "I have no desire to see that *puttana* for as long as I live."

"Closure," Nicholas commented. "Closure for you and for her."

"I got my closure when she cleaned me out," Kieran rolled his eyes, "that was all the closure I needed."

"This is real closure," Eli commented from the back seat. "Face-to-face, no bull."

Kieran quietly seethed from his seat. He didn't want to interact with his ex. He didn't want anything to do with her and the fact she'd been asking about him, made him roll his eyes so hard he thought he was going to be cross-eyed. "Fine," he replied.

"Besides," Tony nodded to the hip-hop beat coming from the radio, "it's okay to see some other titties besides the ones you're currently seeing."

Kieran concentrated on the view outside. "Can somebody please...?"

Nicholas reached over and slapped the back of Tony's head. "Thank you," Eli commented.

****

The Lovely Kitten was a run of the mill strip club located on the outskirts of Staten Island. It catered to the local crowd with the occasional professional athlete or celebrity dropping by. While the Lovely Kitten wasn't considered to be an upscale strip club, it wasn't low-class, nor were most of the girls working there. Besides the obvious eye candy, the club was known for its food and drinks, making it popular with the locals.

"Can I help you, gentlemen?" A blonde with a thick accent approached the guys.

"Yeah, is Cinna here tonight?" Tony asked.

"She sure is, baby," the blonde put a hand on her hip, "she's doing a dance right now but she'll be available in a few minutes."

"Good," Tony got up and gave the blonde some money. "Give half of that to Cinna and tell her she has a client coming in to see her. The other half is for you for your trouble."

The blonde kissed Tony's cheek and winked at him. "Anytime, baby," she walked away and disappeared behind the curtains.

"You have a dance coming up, partner," Tony mentioned to Kieran when he returned from the bathroom.

Kieran didn't want to be face-to-face with his ex and he most certainly didn't want a lap dance from her. "This night keeps getting better."

"She knows you're here," Tony sat next to his brother. He knew he was crossing a line by bringing Kieran to the club and rehashing his painful past but he also knew his brother needed to deal with his past if he was even remotely serious about his future with Tiana. "She's waiting for you behind that curtain."

Kieran sighed. He took a shot of his bourbon and decided it wasn't strong enough. He hadn't planned on drinking anything that night, but a surprise trip to a strip club featuring his ex made him knock back a drink. He quickly got over his anger and irritation. It would be his chance to ask Jalara what she had been thinking when she left him and their future.

Kieran swallowed another sip along with his pride. He then headed behind the curtain.

****

He was gorgeous. Absolutely gorgeous. Thick, dark wavy hair. Muscular build. Strong and wonderful hands, she remembered how they would caress and explore her body when they made love. She could remember how big his cock was and how she loved to ride it over and over and over.

Jalara Stevens smiled at her ex-husband as she walked towards him. If he wanted another go-round with her, she wouldn't even hesitate to fulfill his request. "Welcome back, baby."

Whatever happened to his ex-wife was not pleasant. The time between their divorce and their meeting had not done her any favors. Her face was haggard and the makeup job didn't hide the acne scars and dark circles. Her body, once young and lithe, had aged with considerable weight gain and if Kieran looked closely, some old track marks. The only thing youthful about her appearance was her obvious breast implants.

Her strawberry blonde mane was stringy and her eyes were the most telling—they were lifeless and empty. It was then that Kieran no longer had anger towards his ex. He simply felt sorry for her.

"Jalara," Kieran didn't smile, "how have you been?"

"I've been great," her voice was raspier than Kieran remembered. Jalara always had a smoking habit. "How have you been? Nice to see you around here."

"I'm in town visiting," Kieran cleared his throat. "I'll be leaving soon."

"I'm glad you could stop by," Jalara grabbed Kieran's hand and led him to the couch. She put on some music and dimmed the lights a little. She walked back over to him and straddled his waist. "Did Tony tell you I've been asking about you? He comes in here all the time."

"He told me," Kieran kept his hands to himself.

"Did he tell you I got married again? I just had a baby a few months ago," Jalara ground against Kieran's lap. "I look good for someone who just had a baby, huh?"

Truth to be told, Jalara didn't look good even if she didn't just have a baby. "Your husband doesn't mind you're stripping?" Kieran asked.

"Why would he?" Jalara leaned back on Kieran as she continued to grind on him, "he owns the club."

The word Kieran was thinking of came easily to him. *Magnaccia.* Pimp. "Of course," Kieran replied.

"How have you been?" Jalara peeled off her top and revealed her breasts. "I've heard you've been doing pretty well."

Kieran admired Jalara's breasts. It was the only good thing about her at the moment. "I'm doing fine," Kieran briefly contemplated mentioning Tiana but it was best he kept that news private. There was no need to tell Jalara that information.

"That's good, real good to hear," Jalara turned around and faced Kieran. "You know, not a day goes by that I wonder what could've been between us."

Kieran couldn't tell if Jalara was being honest or blowing smoke up his ass. "So why did you leave?"

Jalara gave a half-hearted shrug as she kept dancing. "I was too young? You were too young? Our marriage was a mistake, Kieran. We probably would've divorced, anyway."

"I understand that part," Kieran replied, "but I don't understand you cleaning me out and taking everything but my clothing and shoes. That's the part I'm having a hard time digesting."

"Kieran," Jalara leaned forward and continued to grind against him, "I needed the money. I knew you were able to make some more and would be okay. I didn't know about my future. I had bills to pay, I was in school. You were off in the military fighting and I barely heard from you when you were gone. I mean, had I known what was going to happen, I would've stayed for sure."

Jalara's admission caught Kieran by surprise. He forced her steady with his hands. "What do you mean had you known what was going to happen, you would've stayed?"

"I mean," Jalara shrugged again, "I mean, your mom did win a lot of money from the lottery."

Kieran's eyes raged with thunderous anger. "Are you seriously telling me that your only regret of us not being together is because you couldn't have any of the lottery winnings? My *mother's* lottery winnings?"

"That's not the only reason," Jalara reasoned.

"But it's the primary one," Kieran forced Jalara off him. "You didn't give a damn about me back then just like you don't give a damn about me now. We're done here." He then left the room.

Kieran made his way back to his brothers. "Everything's done. Let's go. I've had enough entertainment here to last me a long while." He caught a glimpse of Jalara standing outside of her private room. She had a hand on her hip and a seductive smirk on her face. He turned back away from her. "For a *long* while."

The brothers stood up and began to gather their belongings. "Is everything handled?" Nicolas asked.

"Yes," Kieran didn't want to elaborate. He turned back around and saw Jalara bringing another patron into the private room and closed the curtain behind her. "I dodged one helluva of bullet."

TWELVE

"So, Ms. Thang," Faith put the shampoo cape on Tiana, "what can I do for you today?"

"On the floor," Tiana stated matter of fact. "I want all of my hair on the floor."

Faith had been a hairstylist as long as she could remember. She started styling hair back in high school and finally opened her own beauty salon in conjunction with Tony's barber shop. When Tiana requested to get her hair done, Faith jumped on the chance to style the hair of one of the world's most influential women.

Tiana told Faith she wanted a haircut but Faith didn't realize Tiana was actually referring to a big chop. "You can't be serious, Ms. Tiana? Look how long and beautiful your hair is!"

"I need something different and what better way to be different than to cut it all off!" Tiana smiled. "I have a baby son and I don't have the time, or want, to be fixing my hair when I'm chasing him all over the house."

"Girl, I hear that," Faith replied through the mirror. "Short and sexy is the only way to go. Okay, darling, I'll fix you up. How short are we talking?"

Tiana studied Faith's hair through the mirror. "Like yours. I like your cut."

Faith nodded and bent down to Tiana's ear. "It's those D'Amato boys, huh? Have a girl be all twisted up and cutting off her hair and shit," she winked, "I'll hook you up, girl. You're going to be looking so good, Kieran is gonna put it on you tonight!"

****

"How's Staten Island?" Erin asked over the phone. "Are there any gangsters there?"

"Girl, you need to stop watching so much Hollywood," Tiana replied back. "That's how people get in trouble. They see something on TV and think everyone from that group really acts like that."

"Well, am I right? Are his family guidos?" Erin asked.

"Girl, I'm about hang up on you in a minute if you don't quit."

"But for real…his family is cool with you, right?" Erin inquired.

"They are the craziest bunch of people I've met but they are so wonderful," Tiana sat down on the bed. "I mean as an only child, I guess I could never imagine the love and camaraderie between Kieran and his brothers. They all protect and love each other. And the way they acted towards Tyson? Forget it! They simply love and adore him. I mean, I really lucked out with Kieran."

"So you meeting his family, feeling all lucked out…" Erin trailed off.

"Spill it, woman," Tiana sighed.

"That means a trip to your family is in the works, right?" Erin asked.

"It does," Tiana paused, with uncertainty and nervousness. If her mother smarted to Kieran when she knew he was just the help, Tiana could imagine her reaction once she discovered the fact he moved from the guest quarters to her home. "It does."

"Now, one more time with passion and believability, please?"

"I know how my mother is going to act once she realizes that Kieran is no longer just my nanny but also my boyfriend," Tiana already knew her mother's reaction. She was still seething from the union with Christopher.

"So? Why does her opinion matter?"

"Because it always has," Tiana sighed, "you know how she is. Nothing else was or is important as long as she has the last say."

"You really think she'll have that big of an issue with you and Kieran being together?"

"Honestly, yes," Tiana admitted. Her mother was open-minded enough to accept the race difference but that was it. Tiana knew her mother was going to have a *real big issue* with Tiana dating someone who is still on her payroll. "I think she'll get out the Holy Water and rosary beads."

"So, let's say she will be Telenovela dramatic with her reaction, because we both know she will," Erin replied, "what are you going to do about it?"

Tiana thought carefully about her answer. "I'm going to do something I should've done a long time ago—stand up for myself."

"So you say," Erin wasn't as confident as Tiana was, "are you really going to do it?"

"Yes," Tiana held her ground, "I'm a grown woman. I can't have my mother dictate my actions for the rest of my life."

"All righty, then," Erin replied, "just promise me one thing."

"What's that?"

"Make sure all of it is on video. I need proof!"

****

"Where are we going today?" Tiana asked as she climbed into the SUV.

"We're going to a few places around town," Kieran secured Tyson in the car seat and made sure he was bundled up. Joey let him borrow his truck for the day so he could give Tiana a tour of his neighborhood. "Show you a few of my old stomping grounds."

"I'm excited," Tiana smiled, "I get to see more of who you really are."

"As promised," Kieran got inside the truck and started. He kissed his girlfriend for good measure, to her surprise. "No reason, just because."

Kieran drove throughout the city, showing Tiana his old schools, favorite hangouts and even popped by a few old friends' homes to see how they were doing. He haggled with older members of the community about life and sports and a few shared some embarrassing stories about Kieran to Tiana.

After a lengthy tour, the trio stopped by a diner for lunch. "So what do you think so far?" Kieran asked. "I haven't scared you too badly, have I?"

"I love it!" Tiana beamed. "It seemed everyone knew you."

"I helped out a lot around here, plus with me and my brothers, it's pretty hard to forget us due to our sizes," Kieran snacked on a French fry, "but this is a good community with good values."

"I see that," Tiana grabbed his hand and rubbed her thumb on the back of it, "I want you to meet my parents—formally—when we return to California."

Kieran chewed slowly on another French fry. His first encounter with Barbara wasn't what he would call pleasant. There was something about Barbara that really rubbed him the wrong way. The stories Tiana shared with him about her childhood didn't help the already-sour image he had of her parents.

"I will on one condition," Kieran began, "you be you when we go."

Tiana shook her head. "I don't understand."

"You said you were tired of putting on a front. You were tired of being something you're not. Now's your chance. You be you." He sipped his soda. "Whoever she is, that's what you need to be."

"I can't," Tiana took back her hand, "forget I even said anything."

Kieran thought about dropping the subject but he couldn't let it go. "So you're an actress and a runner?"

"Kieran, you don't get it, all right? You don't get it." Tiana shook her head. She hated how strong the feelings were towards the people who gave her life. Her parents seemed to have brought out the very best and worst within her. "I can't just be who I want to be around them. It doesn't work that way."

"Why not?" He asked. "Why is your image so precious to you that it's worth sacrificing your happiness?"

"Because it is, all right?" Tiana said in a tone much louder than she intended. "Because it's all I have left."

Kieran wiped his mouth. "Is it? So that woman from the other night, who told me she was naked and raw and professed her love to me, who was that? Was that the real Tiana Morris or was that her representative?"

"If you want to change your hair, no big deal. If you don't want to take on a new client, no big deal. You've always had support,

Kieran. You've always had someone cheering you on and inspiring you to do your best," Tiana's eyes became watery again. "I haven't always had that."

Kieran grabbed Tiana's hand and held it tight. "Your friends seem very supportive of you, Tiana."

"Exactly, you just nailed it. My *friends*. Not my father and certainly not my mother." The tears began to fall down her cheeks. "And when I announced to them I was leaving Christopher, do you know what their reaction was? Do you even have an inkling of how they reacted? This is how they reacted and quoting, 'Well, that was a waste of money!'"

Kieran held tighter onto Tiana's hand as he tried to quiet his anger. "I'm so sorry, *bella*."

"All of my life, Kieran, all of my life, I've wanted their approval. I wanted them to say, 'Hey, good job!' or 'Way to go, Tiana!' My entire life I've wanted that. I created this image just to make them happy and I still get grief!" She let out a deep, emotional sigh. "So, when I say I don't know if the "real me" is going to show up at my parents' home, I honestly don't know."

Kieran leaned in closer and wrapped his arms around his girlfriend, who softly cried into his chest. "Don't feel you have to pretend with me, okay? You never have to be someone you aren't while we're together."

****

"You know, mamma, you really didn't have to do this for me," Kieran looked around the table.

Nicola pulled out all the stops for her son's birthday. There was food and drink to last for days from the carbonara, spaghetti, and tortellini to all the salad and garlic bread one could handle. In the center of the table was a huge chocolate birthday cake his mother made just for him. His cousins, uncles, and aunts began to pile into his mother's home and even they brought food with them.

"Oh, hush, *il figlio.* Today is your birthday and I always celebrate birthdays, so hush." Nicola announced to all. "Everyone! Everyone, come closer! Kieran is going to blow out his candles now!"

Kieran sat down at the table and looked up at the sight around him. He was surrounded by his brothers, and so many other relatives. The most important sight was seeing Tiana right next to him, holding Tyson. His birthday was extra special that year.

"Well, make a wish!" Nicola cheered. "Hurry up and blow the candles before they spoil my beautiful cake!"

Kieran closed his eyes and made a wish. He then blew out his candles to cheers and camera shots from his family. He stood up and kissed Tiana. "Did you make a good wish?" She smiled.

Kieran grabbed Tyson from her and held them close to him. "I already have what I want."

****

"I'm sure I have a ton of things I need to catch up on," Tiana entered her office and placed her laptop on the dock, "so I'll carefully go through the e-mails later. Anything pressing I need to know?"

"Your hair?" Allison appeared at Tiana's doorway "I love your hair!"

Tiana shook her natural curls a little. The transitioning process had been tougher than she imagined but she knew it would be worth it at the end. She already loved not having the scabs on her scalp from accidentally leaving the relaxer in too long. "Yeah, it's a new style I'm going to keep."

"It looks great. No pressing matters to report on." Allison smiled. "How was Staten Island?"

"It was wonderful!" Tiana beamed. For the first time in ages, she felt she could let her hair down and not have any false pretenses on who she was or what she was about. She'd bonded with Nicola and Faith, who treated her like she'd been a part of the family for years. It was something Tiana needed. "We're going back in a few months."

"In a few months, huh?" Allison folded her arms. "It sounds serious between you two."

"As serious as it can be," Tiana added.

"So, does this mean I'm going to start seeing wedding planner appointments in your calendar?" Allison teased.

"I think you have some work you need to catch up on," Tiana replied back.

After Allison left her office, Tiana got on the phone with her mother. "Hi, Mother. Sorry I didn't call when I got in last night but it was already too late to call."

"I'm glad you're back home and away from the ghetto," Barbara commented.

Tiana rolled her eyes. It was too early to deal with her mother. "I just wanted to check in with you so I'll talk to you later—"

"Christopher has been asking about you," Barbara mentioned. "He's been coming over here a lot."

Barbara's revelation disturbed Tiana in more ways than one. Her ex-husband, who refused to see his child, was making special guest appearances at her parents' home. "Why would my ex be coming around there?"

"He wants to see his son."

"He has my number," Tiana mentioned. "He also knows I don't live there."

"You should applaud Tyson's father for wanting to be a part of his son's life, Tiana," Barbara mentioned over the phone. "He has the ability to be a good father for Tyson."

"He has the ability, he just doesn't want to." Tiana added.

"Nevertheless, he wants to see his son so I invited him over for dinner on Sunday. Bring Tyson along."

"Y-y-you invited him for dinner?" Tiana was astonished. Her mother had lost whatever sense she had left. "Why on Earth would you do that after what I've been through with him?"

"I just told you, and I don't need to justify my actions to my daughter," Barbara replied. "Dinner will be at five-thirty p.m. so I expect to see you over here. I'll talk to you then, Tiana."

Tiana slammed her phone down and felt her fists curl up into tight balls. No matter how good a mood she was in that particular day, it seemed her mother would find that one good nerve of hers and pounce on it.

****

"We have dinner with my mother on Sunday," Tiana began over dinner. Her mood hadn't improved over the day and she took it home with her, something she tried hard not to.

Kieran picked up on Tiana's somber tone. She barely kissed him hello when she arrived home and she was going through the motions when they talked over dinner. "Let's not get excited," Kieran fed Tyson in his high chair.

"I wanted you to meet my parents but not under these circumstances," Tiana played with her mashed potatoes. "Christopher is going to be there."

Kieran nodded as if he accepted the information. He knew the man revered as Champagne Cris and his reputation inside the studio and out. Tiana didn't have to tell Kieran the story about her marriage; it was common knowledge she stayed in much longer than she should have. Still, he respected the fact Tiana had reservations about introducing him to her parents. "I can stay home, Tiana."

"No, I'm not ashamed of you and you're my partner," she declared, "I just wanted to prepare you for what was to come."

"You think it's going to be that bad?" He asked.

"In a word, yes," she replied.

Kieran took off Tyson's bib and removed the high chair table. He then began to burp the infant. "So what's your course of action? Are you going to go there with full artillery or watch carefully and see what happens?"

"I'm going to be packin' like one of those hip-hop ga-ga-gangstas," she then burst into laughter. She walked over to her boyfriend and kissed him and her son. "I can handle my parents. I'm allowed to make my own decisions and not consult them for advice any longer."

"If you don't want to go over there, Tiana, we don't have to."

"And what for? To keep running away from my parents forever? To be this perfect little child who was always seen and never heard? I'm tired of that. I can't promise it'll be a great time but I can't stay away." Tiana picked up Tyson. "It's time to give little man his bath and set him down for the night."

"Did you want me to help?" Kieran offered.

"No, I got this. You rest and relax. I need some mother-son time with Tyson," she smiled back, "I'll take care of you when I'm done." She winked before she left.

Kieran began to clear off the plates and put food away. He knew Sunday's dinner was going to be unforgettable. He just wondered how he was going to react to meeting the infamous Champagne Cris in person.

He would somehow find the urge to resist knocking the man out.

THIRTEEN

Christopher heard through the grapevine that his ex-wife had a new boyfriend. A new boyfriend she didn't want to admit to in public. For weeks, he wondered what he looked like and already assumed everything about the guy.

He concluded Tiana's boyfriend was probably a nerd and weighed a buck-fifty, soaking wet with two bricks. He was probably in the financial sector as well and didn't know any slang and spoke proper English all the time. And knowing Barbara, Tiana's new boyfriend was more than likely a Black man.

So when the mammoth, also known as Kieran, showed up to dinner, Christopher was scared shitless. Kieran was *huge*. His collared Polo barely fit his arms and the hard look on Kieran's face suggested in no way, shape, or form should Christopher even *think* about fucking with him.

"Pleasure to meet you," Kieran extended a hand to Christopher.

Christopher glanced down at Kieran's hand and contemplated if he should shake it. He wasn't too sure Kieran wouldn't break his arm. "Nice to meet you, too, man," he shook his hand. Kieran had a firm grip and Christopher quickly snatched his hand away and massaged it.

He turned his attention to Tiana. She was as beautiful as ever. She recently cut her hair and it was a short do. Way too short for his liking. When they got back together, he would insist she get a weave. "Tiana, darling." He kissed her cheek.

Tiana remained still as fire flashed in her eyes. Christopher had some nerve pretending everything was cool and civil between them, especially after the mud-slinging party he invited her to during their divorce proceedings. She kept her cool. She didn't want to be there, let alone make a scene. "Christopher," she said it in a tone that gave no indication of her feelings one way or another.

Christopher pulled back and admired his ex. "You look absolutely beautiful, Tiana."

"Thank you," she forced a grin, "where are my parents?"

"Your dad is out picking up some liquor for us," Christopher sniffed and rubbed his nose, "your mama is in the kitchen."

"I'll go see her," Tiana headed towards the kitchen.

Christopher looked at Kieran before him. He was holding Tyson and it seemed the boy had a great deal of affection towards his caretaker. "Let's rap for a moment, brah," Christopher walked towards the outside porch. He opened a beer and offered it to Kieran, who politely declined.

"So, you're Kayron, huh?" Christopher sipped his Bud Light.

"Keer-ren," Kieran pronounced his name for the man. He didn't mind the fact his three-year-old nephew had trouble pronouncing his name. He had an issue when a grown man was purposely butchering it.

"Yeah, I said that," Christopher grabbed a cocktail shrimp and slurped on it, "how long have you been with Tiana?"

"A few months," Kieran replied as he coddled Tyson.

"A few months, huh?" Christopher chewed the shrimp, smacking his lips together. "And what is it that you do?"

"I own a child care business," Kieran studied Christopher. He had a goatee and was only a few shades darker than the white tee-shirt he was wearing. His brown hair was closely cropped to his head.

He had an attitude that was half-swagger and half-crap. It was clear he had a Napoleon complex.

Christopher nodded. "That's cool. I guess Tiana already told you what I do for a living?"

"I've heard," Kieran tersely replied.

"Of course you have," a slow smirk formed on the corner of Christopher's lips, "I'm all over the radio."

You were *all over the radio.* Champagne Cris hadn't had a hit in years and it was rumored he was close to being broke due to his lifestyle and extravagant spending. He was notoriously known to wear brand-new white tee shirts every day because he liked the "brand-new" feel. Kieran didn't have to do too much thinking to know where Christopher's intentions lay. He decided to get down to business. "Cris, what do you want from me?"

"I don't want nuttin', man," he shrugged, "I don't want a damn thing."

Kieran tightened his lips and let out a small sigh. Christopher was wasting his time and playing him stupid. "So why are we talking?"

"I'm coming back," Christopher took another swig of beer, "I'm coming back for my family."

Kieran felt his jaw tightened as he held Tyson. There was no way in blue hell he was going to let that happen. "Does Tiana know this?"

"She'll know soon enough," Christopher had a smug smile, "I have backup to support me."

Kieran quickly put two and two together. The dinner Barbara had requested was a ploy to get Tiana to come over with Tyson. Kieran could tell Barbara was being nice to him when he showed up at the front door. He ruined her plans. With him present, Tiana wasn't going to reconcile with Christopher.

Kieran took a sip of apple juice to quiet his rising anger. Holding the infant was the only thing that was saving Christopher from getting his head knocked off. "Is that right?"

"That's right, brah," Christopher took another swig of beer, "don't get comfortable now."

"Quick question," Kieran began, "you say you've come back for your family, right?"

"Yeah, and?" The beer gave Christopher imaginary muscles.

"So why is it that the entire time we've been talking, you never asked to hold your son?" Kieran questioned.

Christopher finished his beer and held out his hands. "Here. Give him to me."

Kieran shook his head. "Oh, I don't think that'll be happening…"

****

Dinner was surprisingly cordial. Tiana and Kieran put on the best their behavior and kept their comments to themselves, despite often smart comments from Christopher. Afterwards, the men met in the family room while Tiana helped her mother in the kitchen.

"You're my daughter's new love interest," Henry Morris stoically said.

"Yes," Kieran focused on the screen ahead of him.

Henry nodded approvingly and didn't say another word for a while. The men sat in silence as they watched the football game before them. Just when Kieran was about to break the ice and offer some conversation, Henry finally spoke again. "Just don't hurt her."

Kieran was startled by Henry's sudden words. He thought the older gentleman was speaking to himself. "What?"

"Don't hurt my baby girl," Henry repeated. "She's been through enough with that last joke of a husband. She doesn't need any more bullshit."

Tyson was bouncing on Kieran's lap and making cooing sounds. "I won't hurt her."

"Good," Henry nodded again. He finally looked over at Kieran and Tyson playing with each other. If Henry didn't know any better, he could've sworn Tyson was Kieran's son. "He loves you."

"I love him back," Kieran laughed at Tyson, who smiled.

"I know what my wife is trying to do and I told her I wanted no part of it," Henry began, "I just wanted to let you know where I stood. I didn't care for Sparkling Bubbly, Alize, whatever he calls himself these days, when they were married and I certainly don't care for him now he's showing back up around the home and act like nothing ever happened."

Kieran remained silent as Henry spoke to him. He thought it was particularly amusing Henry was giving him advice when he wasn't known as husband of the year. He kept his thoughts private.

"But I can tell you love my daughter and you love her son, treating him like he's your own. That's all I want," Henry smiled, "and that's all I want."

It occurred to Kieran that Henry was from the old school of 'Do as I say and not as I do.' "As long as I'm with Tiana, I would always love and protect them both," he stated, "I don't need to go anywhere else."

"Good," Henry sipped on his lemonade.

Christopher soon joined the men in the family room, drinking what appeared to be his third beer already. "Y'all are way too quiet in here! It feels like a damn mortuary," he plopped himself down on another sofa, "liven up a little! Sheesh!"

Henry's eyes moved towards Christopher, then back at the TV screen. "Although I do wish *somebody* would go somewhere else."

****

"You were quiet all evening, Mother," Tiana took out the tea bags and began setting up the tea cups. "Is everything okay?"

"No, everything is not okay," Barbara huffed. "I specifically invited you, not your help, over for dinner tonight. Your nanny could have stayed at home."

It felt like Barbara always found that one nerve of Tiana's and just pounded on it. "Kieran is no longer just my nanny," she calmly replied, "we're also dating."

"Fornicating with the help, huh?" Barbara's words cut to Tiana. "I already knew that. He's changed you. And you're walking around here all jumpy, not prim and proper as a lady should." Barbara had a glance over Tiana's choice of attire. "You're wearing jeans and flip-flops. I'll tell you one thing, you're definitely getting a new nanny because that one isn't working out."

Tiana was used to her mother cutting her down, she brushed the insults aside. But when Barbara began to attack Kieran, it was a new ballgame and Tiana was ready to come out swinging. "You have that much dislike for Kieran that you can't even call him by his name?"

Barbara got out the tea tray and desserts from the refrigerator. "Tyson needs both a mother and a father in his life," Barbara replied.

"He has a mother and a father," Tiana snapped back.

"A father for hire doesn't count," Barbara sternly suggested.

"I have given Christopher plenty of opportunity and reason to be a father to Tyson and he has refused each and every time." Tiana hopelessly explained, "Christopher is more interested in my bank account than what Tyson's favorite toy is. He has not been shy about his feelings."

"You need to try harder," Barbara suggested.

The revelation from Barbara was the beginning of a new relationship between herself and Tiana. "I need to try harder? This is my fault now?"

"You know how Christopher is and you know how men are in general. We always have to carry the extra weight. It's been like that for generations past and it will be like that for generations to come. You deal and move on."

"I did move on," Tiana replied, "I got divorced."

"And speaking of which, if you dated that nice Black man I picked out for you, this would've never happened," Barbara reasoned.

"Oh, so it's both my fault that I got divorced because of my White cheating ex-husband?" Tiana tried to keep her temper under control but it was becoming increasingly difficult. "I know you're not trying to say he cheated on me because he's White?"

"It is bad enough being half of an interracial relationship, what do you think little Tyson is going to experience when he gets older? You have a curly-haired, fair-skinned child with light eyes, Tiana. Do you think the Black kids are going to accept him? Do you think the White kids are going to accept him? What do you think is going to happen with him?"

Tiana felt her jaw tightened and her nostrils flared. "I will teach my son his heritage so he's not confused."

"Oh, I don't think Tyson will be confused," Barbara got out the caramel cakes for dessert, "I think you're the one confused."

"I'm confused?" Tiana questioned. "How am I confused?"

"You're acting so weird lately and I think it's your nanny's fault," Barbara mentioned. "You have never been so mouthy and your hair? What is with your hair? You cut your hair ridiculously short and curly, looking like a boy lost in the wilderness. I need to book Eva to fix that mess. You go with him to visit his family in the ghetto. I know what Staten Island is like and it's not pretty. Furthermore, you should've stayed here and tried to fix your marriage. It would've been better for you than to travel across the country with some guy who's not even on your level."

That last comment sent Tiana over the edge. "Funny how I'm getting advice from someone who has an adulterous husband who doesn't give two shits about his wife or his only daughter. You're the queen of keeping up appearances and you're telling me I need to straighten up my act?"

"Now, you watch your mouth, young lady…"

"No, I'm not watching my mouth. I've been watching my mouth my entire life. I've been watching what I eat. I've been watching what I wear. I've been watching how I style my hair. My whole damn life has been about pleasing you! Making you happy! You never asked me what I wanted. You never asked me what I thought. It's always been about you and this fake-ass image. We're not the Huxtables, Mother! Dad is not Cliff and you most certainly are not Claire! I'm tired of being something I am not. I am tired of pleasing people who don't care about how I feel. I'm tired of eating this bland and beige diet to stay trim. For fuck's sake, I like salt!" Tiana let out a sigh of relief. "Kieran has been more of a father to Tyson for the past six months than Christopher ever has been. You know why Christopher has been coming around lately, mother? It's because he's broke! He went through the divorce settlement already. He's been nice and charming, hoping to score some money or a car out of it. You think Christopher cares about you? How many times did he call you when we were married? How many times did he check up on you when we were divorcing? Did you ever wonder why you were the one watching Tyson and not him?

"And now, all of a sudden, when he's broke and damn near destitute, he's coming around like he's the prodigal son and you honestly think he's being truthful? That man wouldn't know what the truth was if he found her on the stripper pole!" Tiana straightened her shirt out. "I've gotten more love from Kieran's mother and she doesn't know me from dirt! She didn't criticize me, she didn't tell me what I was doing wrong, but you know what she did instead? She gave me *encouragement*, something you never have!

"Now I'm about to go home with my boyfriend and you know what we're going to do? We're going to have a nice big-ass piece of pie with ice cream! Good-night!"

****

"You stood up to your mother back there," Kieran warmed up the pie slices in the microwave, "I'm impressed."

Tiana nodded. After the confrontation with her mother, it was best that all three went home. She felt better already without being under her mother's watchful eyes. "It was several years in the making," Tiana took out the vanilla bean ice cream and some forks. "I'm just tired of the judgment and the crap."

"How long have you been putting up with it?" Kieran took out the pies.

"For as long as I can remember," Tiana scooped out some ice cream and put it on the pie slices, "Tiana, do this. Tiana, do that. My mother actually wanted me to go by my middle name, Elizabeth, because she thought Tiana sounded too ethnic."

"So how did she take your marriage to Chris?"

"She hated it and let me know whenever she could, which was often. She said it would've been better if I married a White European because at least Europeans are more cultured," Tiana rolled her eyes, "but Christopher showered her with bling and gifts and well, money talks."

Kieran knew he was walking a fine line with the next question. A part of him wanted to know where he stood with her. A large part wanted to know where *she* stood with him, parental influence or not. "You know why he was there tonight?"

"I know," Tiana replied, more curtly than she intended, "but I also know what I want and Christopher is not in my future plans. He didn't care about me back then and I doubt he cares now. I saw how he was around Tyson tonight; he barely acknowledged him. He nursed his beers more than he played with his son. All he did was solidify my decision to divorce him when I did."

A small silence formed between the pair as Kieran took a bite of his cherry pie. He took notice of how different Tiana's demeanor was when she was on Staten Island, to just a short while ago with her parents. It was a night and day. "So how do you feel now?"

"I feel like I have a pair of diamond-encrusted balls all of a sudden," Tiana beamed. Her shoulders dropped. Dropping all of the weight she'd carried throughout the years made her relaxed and stressed-free. "I feel like I just climbed Mount Everest."

Kieran took another bite of pie and licked his lips. There was a sensuous air between them. "You want to climb something else tonight?"

Tiana scooped a bite of pie and licked the crust of it, before taking it in her mouth, causing a moan from Kieran. "How do you want me, baby?" She seductively asked.

Kieran felt his cock stir in his jeans. He wanted Tiana in many positions, her body twisted in so many ways. He scooped a little ice cream with a finger and smeared it over Tiana's chest. He leaned down to lick the ice cream. "You're dirty," he murmured, "We have to get you clean."

Kieran's tongue was magical and he sent her body into overdrive. He knew how to get her aroused without even saying a word. "You want me in the shower?" She moaned.

Kieran removed his shirt as Tiana took hers off as well. "I want you however I can get you."

Tiana grabbed Kieran's hand and led him to the open air shower in her huge bathroom. She locked eyes with his as she began to unbuckle his belt. She pulled down the jeans along with Kieran's boxer briefs, his thick cock jutting out in anticipation. Her tongue quickly darted out to wet her lips and she softly bit them. She wanted to savor the moment for as long as she could.

She began to take off her jeans when Kieran stopped her. "No," he stepped closer to her, "allow me." He undid the jeans and pulled down the zipper. He slid the jeans along with her panties over her hips and pooled them at her feet.

Tiana carefully stepped out of jeans and waited for Kieran's next direction. She felt his hands slide up and down her body, pausing where her thighs met. He nudged them slightly apart and felt how wet she was. "Damn, *bella*," Kieran murmured, his low rumble vibrating throughout the room. He played with her swollen nub with his thumb, gauging her reaction with every stroke.

She didn't care about her parents. She didn't care about what other people thought. All she wanted was Kieran on her body, hovering over her as he slid in and out of her tight channel. She felt the moisture pooling at her heat, her pussy contracting again. "Baby…" she warned.

"Shh…" Kieran quieted her. He stopped playing with her and led her to the shower. They washed each other's bodies and snuck in kisses. Kieran sat down on a nearby bench in the shower and pulled Tiana on top of him. He adjusted her position and slipped inside her, causing Tiana to slightly yelp at the increased pressure. She sat all the way down on his cock, happily accepting all of him inside her.

Tiana slowly rocked her body against Kieran's, wrapping her arms around his neck. She increased her movement and opened her thighs wider to accommodate him. He fit perfectly inside, completely filling her. "Fuck me, baby…" she moaned.

Kieran grabbed Tiana's ass and guided her. His breath quickened as he approached his own orgasm. "You want to cum?" Kieran kissed Tiana's neck. "You want to cum on my dick?"

"Fuck, baby," Tiana rode him faster. Her body stilled as the orgasm shot through her body, Kieran soon following her. She collapsed on top of him, showering him with kisses. "Baby, I love you."

"I love you, too, *bella*."

FOURTEEN

"What about this one?" Tiana walked over to a big tree at the lot. "I like this one!"

It seemed the holidays sprang upon them in record time. They had a nice Thanksgiving with Tiana's friends and it was just a few days before Christmas. They already started planning more trips to back to Staten Island during the next year.

Kieran held Tyson as he walked over to the pine tree at the Christmas tree lot. It was a nice tree but he wasn't sure about it. "I don't know. It doesn't have that 'umph' to it."

"That *umph*?" Tiana teased. "I didn't think Christmas trees had 'umphs.'"

"They do," Kieran caressed the pine needles. "You have to find the right one."

"I have found the right one. I found the right one about five times, already," she replied, "I'm tired of finding the right one."

"It's because you're not seeing it how I'm seeing it," Kieran walked with her to another tree, "you see a tree that has sturdy branches and fir to put some dangling ornaments. I see memories. I see which branch is going to have the first ornament. I see Tyson's face lighting up when he crawls to the tree, plays with said ornaments, and is amazed by seeing them fall on the floor." He wrapped his free arm around Tiana, "I see us snuggling up against the fireplace and admiring the lights."

Tiana smiled. "This is the tree?"

"This is the tree," Kieran nodded. "Let's get this one."

"Okay, stay right here so no one else gets it! I'll get someone else to help us!" Tiana ran off.

Kieran pulled out his phone and glanced at his incoming message. He got a voicemail from the jeweler; Tiana's engagement ring was ready. It was going to be a Christmas neither one would ever forget.

"Okay, this is the tree!" Tiana instructed to the guy next to her. "We'll take this one." She watched as the man took the tree and prepared it for Kieran's truck. She turned to Kieran. "Is everything okay? I saw you on your phone just now."

"Just checking messages," he warmly smiled to her. "Just checking messages."

After the trio left the tree lot, they went straight home and decorated the tree. Tiana put Tyson to bed and re-joined her boyfriend in the living room with the crackling fire place and lit Christmas tree. She snuggled with Kieran and lay on his chest. "This is what Heaven is like."

"I think so," Kieran rubbed Tiana's arm. "I couldn't have asked for a better Christmas gift."

"I'm sure you want a nice Christmas gift, baby?" she asked. "Don't you want an upgrade to another bike? Or a better SUV?"

"I thought about it, but I'm good. I don't ride on the bike as much as I should, so it doesn't have that many miles on it. My truck is fine; I just need to get it serviced one of these days," Kieran shrugged, "I don't really need anything."

Tiana turned to face him. "You are probably the only man I have ever met who didn't want something for Christmas?"

There was something Kieran wanted for Christmas—a *yes* from Tiana. He would have to wait until Christmas Day to get it. "It's not that I don't want *anything*," he clarified, "it's just everything I have is here. But if you insist on giving me something, you can buy me clothing."

"Clothing?" Tiana questioned. "That's an unusual request. Why clothing?"

"Because eventually all women change their man's clothing. It may not be right away but it's a gradual step. A tie here. A shirt there. Some new socks here. Some new underwear there. Next thing I know, I have a wardrobe full of brand-new clothes and I had no idea what happened to my lucky Steelers jersey," Kieran shook his head as Tiana giggled, "you know I'm right?"

"I promise I won't mess with your lucky Steelers jersey," Tiana crossed her heart.

"Oh, you better not," Kieran warned, "you can do whatever you want to my clothes but if you mess with that jersey, woman, we will be fighting."

Tiana snuggled again with him. "What is it with guys and their lucky jerseys?"

"Hey, whether the Steelers win depend on that jersey," Kieran pointed out. "If I wear it, they win. If I don't wear it, they don't win."

"Ooh, so that means you haven't been wearing your jersey that much lately, huh?" Tiana smiled.

"Touché, *bella*. Touché." Kieran laughed. "So what do you want for Christmas?"

"You know, every year I never wonder what I want. I spend all this money on my friends and family, making sure they're happy, but I never wonder what *I* want. I'm more focused on making sure

Tyson has a great Christmas than on any gift I might hope for," Tiana slightly shrugged, "so honestly, I don't want anything for Christmas."

"I'll give you something," Kieran rubbed her arm, "I have a gift in mind."

"Oh, you do?" Tiana became intrigued. "What is it?"

"Do you want to know now or wait until Christmas?" Kieran replied. He was really hoping she would wait until Christmas.

"You know what? I'll wait." Tiana smiled. "It's more fun to wait."

Kieran breathed a small sigh of relief. "I think so, too."

****

"So do you and Kieran have big plans for Christmas?" Allison inquired.

"We're going to stay in town for a little while and then we're heading back to Staten Island to ring in the New Year," Tiana couldn't wait. She had gotten tired of celebrating the New Year, going to the same boring parties with the same boring people. This year was going to be extra special with Kieran and his family. Being an only child, she loved the pandemonium of Kieran's large family and the multitude of personalities. Even if someone had a beef with another person, they always put it aside as long as Nicola served some of her famous tortellini.

"Sounds pretty serious between you two?" Allison prodded.

"You said that the last time?" Tiana replied.

"And am I right? Is it not serious?" Allison asked.

Tiana tried to hide the big smile that was forming. "Maybe," she replied.

"Yeah, *maybe* my tail!" Allison laughed.

"Listen, it's not that…" Tiana's phone rang and she picked up her phone. "Hold that thought, Allison. Yes? This is Tiana Morris, how can I help you?" Tiana listened intently on the phone. Her eyes narrowed and fine lines formed in the crease of her forehead. "What? I'll be right there. Thank you."

"What's going on?" Allison asked.

"Something happened to Christopher and he's at the hospital. I'll be out for the rest of the day. Take all of my calls and just let everyone know I'll be back in tomorrow," she rushed out the door.

When Tiana arrived at the hospital, she made her way to Christopher's room. When she entered his room, she was astonished by what she saw. Two long tubes were hanging from his mouth and nose. A needle was in his arm and attached to an IV. He was ten shades paler than she had ever seen him.

She swallowed the lump in her throat as a nurse stood beside her. "Are you the wife?" She asked.

"Ex," Tiana corrected, "ex-wife."

"He had a nice cocktail of Xanax, cocaine, and roofies which he washed down with alcohol," The nurse stated as she checked his breathing machine. He was stable enough to have the tubes removed. "He's lucky he's even alive."

Tiana's mind was clouded with confusion. As much anger she had for the man, she didn't want anything to happen to the father of her child. "When did this happen?"

"Just a few hours ago. He partied all night and his friends claim they don't know what happened to him." The nurse rolled her eyes. "They all say that when they don't want to get into trouble."

Tiana kept her eyes on Christopher. She was distressed by his state; there were tubes everywhere and he looked nothing like what he did when she last saw him. She was angry at seeing him; how dare he do drugs and party when he had an infant son who needed his father? She was relieved he was still alive; maybe it could give him a second chance at life to start over. "Okay. Thank you."

The nurse walked away and Tiana closed the door behind her. She walked into the hospital room and pulled up a chair next to Christopher's bed. She grabbed his hand and softly kissed it. For several hours, she kept vigil at his bedside and thought about their marriage.

She thought about their wedding day again and how they promised forever and eternity to each other. She thought about how they were trying to have a baby and how frustratingly long it took them to finally conceive. She thought about Tyson's birth and how Christopher had tears of joy that he finally had a son.

Tiana then thought about the screaming matches they would have with each other. She thought about the numerous women who would crank call her phone at all hours of the night. She thought about Christopher's open flirtations with other women right in front of her face. And then her last memory of Christopher right before their divorce proceedings—how she caught him in bed, their bed, with another woman. She knew Christopher was cheating on her and the gossip blogs were full of lurid details about him sleeping with this singer and that singer. But for Tiana to actually see it with her own eyes? She had no choice but to leave.

Looking back at Christopher, Tiana briefly wondered if her leaving him somehow contributed to his demise. "Damn you," she muttered under her breath.

"What did I do now?" Christopher opened his eyes.

Tiana was startled by Christopher's voice. "You're alive," she commented.

"I had a boo-boo," Christopher replied.

"I'm glad you're okay," Tiana stood up. "I'll be leaving now."

"Tiana, wait," he called after her, making Tiana pause. "I want us to be a family," Christopher pleaded, "like old times?"

The revelation made Tiana silently scoffed. *Like old times? Like how you cheated on me left and right? Like how you almost bankrupted me? What glorious old times are you thinking, fool?* The state of Christopher's health made her bite her tongue. "What do you need from me, Christopher?" She didn't turn around to face him.

"I want to move back home," he coughed, "I want us back together. The three of us."

"Why, Christopher?" Tiana finally turned around. "Why? So I can support your drug habits? So you can entertain your groupies? So I can be made a laughing stock again? Why, Christopher?"

"Because I got a second chance at life, TeeTee. I got a second chance at *us*," Christopher pleaded. "Yeah, I'll admit I was an asshole. I'll admit I mistreated you. I'll admit all of that. But I'm also willing to admit that I believe in second chances and I want you to give me one."

Christopher wasn't asking for too much; he was asking for *everything*. If Christopher moved back home, there was no way Tiana could keep a relationship with Kieran. Kieran wouldn't have any part of it and she couldn't blame him. It was a decision between what was best for her—and what was best for her son. *Tyson needs his father.*

"Okay," Tiana softly replied. She knew just by uttering that one word, she was making the biggest mistake of her life.

Breaking the news to Kieran was going to be the toughest part.

****

"You have been quiet all evening," Kieran said over dinner, "is everything okay?"

Tiana asked Erin to babysit Tyson so she and Kieran could go out to dinner. She took him to a high-profile restaurant and asked him to dress accordingly. She had a single glass of wine and chewed her food slowly. Her stomach was tightly coiled and no matter how much water she drank, she couldn't escape the dryness of her throat.

Kieran didn't pay any attention to what Tiana was doing. He was nervous himself. He wanted to wait until Christmas to propose but decided it was best to do it Christmas Eve. He wanted them to enjoy Tyson's first Christmas together and let Tiana have her own night. He lightly patted his sweaty forehead and had water instead of any alcoholic beverage. He wanted to remember this night.

"Um…" Tiana quickly swallowed her food and took a sip of wine. She braced herself for Kieran's reaction. Was he going to be emotionless and respectful? Would he toss a table over and scream obscenities? She could only hope for the former and definitely not the latter. "There is something I do need to talk to you about."

"Oh?" Kieran felt the ring box chafing his slacks. He was growing increasingly anxious by the minute. "What's on your mind, *bella?*"

The next few minutes were a blur to Kieran. It seemed everything paused in slow motion as he listened intently to what Tiana said to him. He paid very close attention to her lips. *"I got a call he was in the hospital…"*

All he heard was noise even though he could understand Tiana just fine. *"He begged and cried for another chance…"*

He watched her lips and thought he saw them tremble in nervousness. *"I decided Tyson needed his father…"*

He read her eyes; she was apologetic and remorseful, hoping that he would understand her point of view.

"I want to let you know it wasn't an easy decision and it wasn't one I took lightly," Tiana continued, "but Christopher wants to be a father to Tyson and have another chance at working things out so…" her voice trailed off.

Kieran looked at her, emotionless. His face darkened and he remained silent for a long while. He reached over took a sip of her wine, then finished it. "Thank you," he got up to leave.

"Kieran," Tiana called out after him, "I would like for us to still be friends?"

The admission caused Kieran to stop walking. He rubbed his mouth in frustration, unbelievable that his ex had the audacity to ask such a request. He turned around. "That's what you would like? You would like us to be friends?"

Tiana nodded. "I would."

Kieran walked back to her and looked down at her with an icy glare. "You know what I would like, Tiana? I would've liked to have been your husband. I would've liked to have been a father to Tyson and possibly adopt him. I knew from the moment I met you, I was in love with you. I knew it right then and there. And I broke a rule getting involved with you. I broke the only rule I have ever followed and that is not to get too involved with a client and their family.

"You do what makes you happy, Tiana." He reached inside his pocket and pulled out a ring box. He opened it up and set it down in front of her. In front of Tiana was a sparkling two-carat diamond solitaire ring. "This was going to be yours tonight. I wasn't satisfied with just being your boyfriend and I wanted more. Maybe you did me a favor." Kieran kissed her forehead. "But us being friends? If I can't be your husband, I most certainly won't be your friend. You can keep the ring." He then left the restaurant.

FIFTEEN

"So have you heard from Kieran lately?" Rocio asked over lunch.

Tiana shook her head. She wished she heard from him. The same night she broke up with Kieran, he packed up his belongings and slept in the guest house. By the next morning, he was gone. She called him so he could get his last paycheck from her but he never replied. Instead, his assistant called her back to let Tiana know she could mail the check to the office. The memory made Tiana's heart crumble. Kieran was so heartbroken, he didn't even want to *speak* to her.

She found herself visiting the Fits and Giggles website on a semi-hourly basis just to see his picture. Tyson's first Christmas was somber and Tiana barely remembered New Years. It was already time for Erin's January wedding.

"So the best thing that's ever happened to you walked out the door because the worst thing that's ever happened to you wanted a second chance?" Erin asked. "Is that what I'm understanding?"

"You don't understand my situation, Erin," Tiana replied, "unless you've been in it, you can't understand it."

"One has nothing to do with the other," Erin replied, "the only reason why you're giving Christopher a second chance is because you found him in a drunk and drugged-out state. Had you not found him like that, you would have *never* given him the time of day again."

"Christopher was in a state where he needed me and Tyson. I did what had to be done," Tiana said.

"Yes, because being Champagne Cris's wife has more privilege than being the wife of a child daycare owner," Erin sharply replied, "I totally get it."

The admission caused an air of tension between the best friends. "I don't know why I even try to make you understand, because you simply don't get it." Tiana quietly replied.

"Then help me understand?" Erin asked. "What is it that I don't get? Is it the part that he left you alone to raise Tyson? Is it the part he demanded millions of your fortune but said nothing about seeing his son? Is it the part he tried to weasel his way back to you through your mother? Is it the part he cheated on you left and right before *and* during your marriage? What part of it don't I understand, TeeTee? Please? Because I'm curious!"

"My son's father wants a second chance to make it right for him, for our son, for all of us! Yes, I think Christopher was a shit father and an equally shit husband! Yes, I wish he had turned around before the divorce and legal battles." Tiana stood up for her actions. "And you're damn straight, I wish Christopher had made an effort long before Kieran came into the picture! But he didn't! I did what was best for my son and all involved."

"No, you did what was best for Tiana and *no one* involved," Erin folded her arms. "You don't give a goddamn about anyone but Tiana. You would rather stay in a loveless and lonely marriage than admit you have a dog husband. You would rather have your parents beat you down than grow some balls and tell them to mind their own damn business. You are the *queen* of keeping up appearances and you learned that from your mother. Now, you had a man who accepted you as you are, didn't try to change you, loved and took care of your son as if he was his own, and you left him to give your shit ex another chance because you thought that was the best course of action? Girl, bye!" Erin got out her car keys. "I'm going home because I don't want to be around this train wreck anymore. My wedding is on Saturday and the rehearsal is on Friday. I'll see you then." She then left.

A small silence passed between Tiana and Rocio. "You know she has a point, TeeTee," Rocio quietly spoke.

Tiana sipped her water and let out an angry breath. "So both of my best friends think I'm an idiot? Great."

"TeeTee, we saw how happy you were with Kieran. We haven't seen you that happy in a long time," Rocio reached over and grabbed Tiana's hand, "you know I will support you no matter what happens. But I'm not going to lie, TeeTee. I think you made a big mistake."

"Well, what's done is done," Tiana replied, "What's done is done."

"Speaking of Christopher, where is he?" Rocio asked. "I haven't seen him around lately."

"He's been busy," Tiana replied. That was the canned response she gave anyone who had asked. Truth was shortly after Christopher came home from the hospital, he took off to New York to supposedly work on an album. He borrowed money from Barbara for studio time and made frequent trips between California, New York, and Miami. He was currently at home watching Tyson before he had to catch another flight the next day.

"Busy, huh?" Rocio smirked. "I'm not even going to comment."

"So, don't." Tiana sharply replied. She took a sip of water and played with her salad. "He's at home watching Tyson and he's making a better effort than he was the last time around."

"Well, I guess anything is a step-up from absolutely nothing," Rocio smiled.

After the lunch, Rocio and Tiana drove back to Tiana's house to finish up the final details of Erin's wedding. They pulled up to Tiana's home and saw an unfamiliar car in the driveway.

"Expecting somebody?" Rocio asked.

"I have no idea who the hell that is," Tiana parked her car and got out of it. She entered her home. "Christopher? Cris?"

"Hello?" A young woman holding Tyson greeted Tiana.

Tiana walked over and snatched Tyson out of her hands. "And who are you?"

The young woman smiled at Tiana with a hand out; Tiana didn't return the courtesy. "I'm Tanya."

"That's nice, but, who the hell are you?" Rocio interrupted.

"I'm a friend of Cris'!" She giggled. "He let me watch the baby while he was gone."

"How long has he been gone?" Tiana asked.

"Only a few hours!"

Tiana's eyes grew wide. "A few hours?" She left for the final bridal fitting that morning and Cristopher was just waking up.

"Just a few! He said he'll be back soon, though." Tanya grabbed her purse. "I guess you're the one who's going to pay me? Cris said you were going to handle it when you came back."

"I'm going to handle something, all right," Tiana folded her arms, "If you don't get out of my house and out of my face within the next five seconds, I will hand you your ass on a platter."

****

"Three came before, but only one came back," Nicola washed the dishes, "want to fill me in on what happened?"

After the sudden break-up with Tiana, Kieran took an extended leave from work and went back to Staten Island to visit his family for a few weeks. He needed to recharge his batteries. He hated, absolutely hated, how a woman could mess up his concentration. He specifically made it a rule not to care and he was always caught up in caring. If only he could be a player like his younger brothers…"We broke up," Kieran replied, "simple as that."

"So you say," Nicola rinsed off a plate and set it in the drying rack, "but was it?"

"I moved out and moved on," Kieran added sugar to his too-hot coffee, "and so did she."

Nicola glanced over at her son. She was convinced that out of her five sons, Kieran was the most sensitive. It was no surprise to her that he opened a child care instead of going into the family business. "I take it that it wasn't your fault?"

"Actually, it was," Kieran took a sip of coffee, "I should've never broken my personal rule."

"Rule schmule," Nicola shook her head, "you can't help who you fall in love with, *il figlio*."

"Actually, you can," Kieran countered, "You can always stop a situation if you know no good will come out of it."

"You could do that. And you could be alone and lonely with several cats like your *Zia* Antonia," Nicola shook her head, "I'm just waiting for her to come out of the closet, already."

"I'd rather not talk about it anymore," Kieran huffed. "She made her decision and that's that. We both moved on."

"If you say so, *il figlio*," Nicola finished the dishes and rinsed off her hands, "but the heart wants what the heart wants."

"Yeah, well, my heart wants something it can't have," Kieran replied back.

Nicola walked up to her son and put a hand on his forearm. "Remember when I dreamt about rainbows, when all three of you were here last time?"

It was a memory Kieran would rather forget. "Yes."

"A dream deferred is not a dream denied," she tapped his arm, "think about it."

SIXTEEN

Looking around at the frantic mood in the hotel room, Tiana remembered her own wedding day all too well. She remembered how much of a nervous wreck she was. She had jittery butterflies in her stomach all day. Come to think of it, it might have been a sign she was making the biggest mistake of her natural born life. The wedding day went *too* perfectly. There was not a distraction or hiccup in sight. Tiana knew why that was the case; she was way too anal retentive to let anything interfere with her wedding day.

In contrast to Erin's wedding, there were already signs of it not going well. The shoes Erin wanted to wear were going to be delivered two days after the wedding, forcing her to get other shoes at the last minute. The hair stylist magically disappeared and no one was able to get in contact with him for hours. There was a major rain storm causing them to move their outdoor wedding indoor. Tiana simply smiled at the differences. It reminded her of the old wives' tale about weddings: the more disasters in a wedding, the happier the impending marriage.

Erin knocked back a shot of vodka. "Girl, I can't wait until this day is over! I've been planning this wedding for the past year and I'm just done! So done! I don't want to go to another cake-tasting, I don't want to see any more coloring shades, I don't want to be on another fucking diet to fit into this damn gown," Erin sighed, "this is fucking it. If Michael doesn't like it, too damn bad. His ass is stuck with me for the rest of his life."

"Come on, it's not that bad," Rocio waddled over to Erin and helped with her hair.

"Yes, it is that bad!" Erin huffed as a family member fixed her hair. "All this planning and plotting for one day. One day! I should've gotten married at the damn courthouse."

"But you didn't," Rocio smiled through the mirror, "the time before the wedding is the worst. You remember my wedding? I couldn't even think straight! And let's not forget about that one over there!" She pointed to Tiana. "She was so drill sergeant, she should've had a second career in the Army."

"I wasn't that bad, was I?" Tiana asked.

"Oh, yeah," Erin remembered. "I had to wear heels the entire night. I remember the rules," She cleared her throat and spoke in an authoritative tone. "You will not get pregnant or you will be out of the wedding. You will not cut your hair or you will be out of the wedding. You will not gain weight or you will be out of the wedding. You will wear your heels throughout the entire night. You never did pay for my bunion surgery, you cheap bastard."

"Hey, I got you a very nice wedding gift in the form of an all-expense paid honeymoon, thank you very much," Tiana smiled back, "you don't have to accept it."

"You know my bunions aren't that bad," Erin replied.

Tiana yawned and grabbed her stomach. How could she be incredibly hungry and sleepy at the same time? "Well, if you're almost ready, I'll head out to the hallway to get in line for the processional."

"Actually, TeeTee," Erin spoke to her in the mirror, "can I talk to you alone for a minute?"

Tiana waited for everyone to leave the room so it was just her and Erin alone. "Yes?"

Erin turned around. "Listen, I'm not going to apologize for what happened the other day. Maybe I was a bit foolish in how I acted, but my intentions were true. While I still think breaking up with Kieran was by far the dumbest thing you could've done, I respect the fact you wanted Tyson to have his father in his life. And if you're happy, I'm happy."

Tiana grabbed her girlfriend's hand and held it. "I always knew you had my back, Erin. But sometimes you need me to make these stupid mistakes on my own," she sighed, "trust me, okay? I'll deal with Christopher whenever he decides to make himself available."

"Whenever he decides to make himself available?" Erin replied. "You know what? I don't even want to know. This is my day and I don't need to hear about ignorant fools messing up my wonderful day. Let's go. We have a wedding to get to."

Tiana joined other members in the wedding party waiting in the foyer of the church. She began to feel light-headed and was convinced it was because the foyer was so crowded, in addition to the air-conditioning not being on. She interlocked arms with her escort and started down the aisle.

Her head began to perspire and her vision was becoming fuzzy. She blinked several times to somehow correct it but it was still no use. What was happening to her?

Tiana took a few more steps and collapsed in the middle of the aisle. It was the last thing she would remember.

****

Tiana slowly opened up her eyes. Where was she? She was at the hospital. She could recognize that smell. It smelled of sanitation and death. She looked towards her left arm. There was a nice needle and accompanying IV bag.

She couldn't remember what happened. "I was wondering when you were going to wake up," Barbara's upbeat voice rang in her ears. She held her right hand and softly smoothed her thumb over it. "You had me worried for a minute."

"I don't know what happened." Tiana softly spoke. "How did I end up in the hospital?"

"You fainted at Erin's wedding. They couldn't revive you at the hotel so they called for an ambulance and brought you here."

Tiana immediately became embarrassed. She ruined her girlfriend's wedding. "Erin hates me," Tiana frowned.

"Quite the opposite, really," Barbara added, "she's very, very concerned for you."

"Who told you I was here?" Tiana asked.

"I got a call from the hospital telling me to come, so here I am," Barbara continued to rub Tiana's hand. "I'll stay until you want me to leave."

Tiana thought about how Barbara would know. She then remembered how she listed her as the first contact in case something ever happened to her or Tyson. "I don't want you to leave," Tiana blurted. "I want you to stay."

Barbara thought about her appearance at the hospital. She was merely keeping Christopher's spot warm until he showed up, whenever that was. "I'll stay as long as I need to."

"Well, Good Morning," the doctor entered in Tiana's room. "I'm glad to see you're awake finally."

"How long was I out, doctor?" Tiana asked.

"Just a few hours. We ran some tests on you while you were passed out so we got all the information we needed about what's going on with you," The doctor pulled up a chair.

Tiana held Barbara's hand tight. "Yes?"

"You need to take it easy from work. Your blood pressure is sky high and you just need to relax. Also, start drinking more water and eat more fruits and vegetables," the doctor instructed.

"You're telling me generics but not giving me the diagnosis," Tiana replied, "what's wrong with me?"

"You're pregnant," the doctor smiled, "seven weeks to be exact." He looked at Tiana's and Barbara's faces. "I see you two have a lot to discuss. I'll be back in later to check up on you, Tiana." He then left the room.

The air was thick with silence for a long while. "I hope I'm right in my assumption that Kieran is the one that got you pregnant and not Christopher?" Barbara began.

Tiana braced herself for her mother's lecture. Not only did she get pregnant with someone her mother considered to be below her level, she was also having a child out of wedlock. It was a double whammy, no matter what side of the coin she looked at it. There was no positive flip side.

"It's Kieran's baby," Tiana mumbled.

Barbara was silent. It was the uncomfortable, condescending silence Tiana was used to. Her mother didn't have say a word to let Tiana know how disappointed she was in her. Tiana was grateful her parents didn't believe in abortion for she knew that would've been the first suggestion her mother would've made.

"I was wrong," Barbara's words broke the silence.

Tiana swore she was hearing things. Did her unforgiving mother actually admit she was wrong? That woman *never* admitted to being wrong—ever. "What?"

"I wanted you to get back with that joke ex-husband of yours because I thought Tyson needed a mother and a father. I wanted you to provide a stable home environment for him, thinking having his natural father was a better option. I was wrong. Christopher is nothing but a sperm donor. I gave him some money to help him out with his music production business and I have yet to get a return on my investment. I not-so politely told him if he comes back around my home again, I would sick my dogs on him," Barbara huffed and Tiana smiled, "My point is, I saw how Kieran was with Tyson. And I saw how he was with you. He made you smile more. He's been a great influence on Tyson. And I'm sure this new baby you two will have will be just as beautiful."

Tiana held back her tears. She had wanted this moment from her mother for as long as she could remember. "That means a lot, Mom."

"I just want my baby happy," Barbara held Tiana's hand, "yeah, I may not agree with all of your choices and yeah, some of the things you do might irritate me to no end, at times, but I just want you to be happy. I'll get over it." Tiana opened her arms out and Barbara leaned in for a hug. "I love you, Tiana."

"I love you, too, Mommy."

"Now," Barbara wiped her tears, "I'm going to get some coffee. I'm going to Coffee Bean because the coffee here at the hospital isn't worth a lick of salt. I want you to think about what you're going to do about your baby and Kieran. I'll be back soon." She then left the room.

Tiana didn't know what she was going to do. She was pregnant. Little Tyson was finally going to have a brother or sister close to his age. She thought about the timing. She and Kieran had only been broken up for a month and Christopher left as soon as he came back. She had been running around so much, she didn't pay attention to her cycles and thought she was just sick and tired because of her schedule.

Now she had to convince the baby's daddy to come back home.

SEVENTEEN

Kieran pulled up to the Elite Realty agency and got out of his truck. Since moving out of Tiana's home, he'd moved back into the extended-stay hotel he was previously staying at. He finally decided it was time for him to find a home of his own. Something with a nice front yard with a fence, a big back yard to host parties and if it had a pool, it was a bonus. Something close to his business and centered where his clients were.

The home search was also a fresh start for Kieran. He needed to do something other than sit around and mope about Tiana all day. He dated other people but it was mainly to have someone in his bed for the night. It was the cycle he went through with Jalara and other girlfriends but the pain was worst with Tiana. He missed her. Furthermore, he missed Tyson. He'd treated the young boy as if he was his own and looked forward to being the father Kieran never had.

He would never break that personal rule again.

"Kieran," Rocio greeted him with a big smile and hug, "I'm glad you came today."

"Rocio?" Kieran was surprised to see her. "What are you doing here?"

"I own this place," she smiled, "I've been a realtor since before I got married to Rashad. In fact, showing him a house is how we met. I can't just be some NBA wife who stays at home, now?"

"I guess not. You could always join the reality shows," Kieran smirked.

"Yeah, and my husband would really *kick* my ass," Rocio laughed.

Kieran smiled back. Though his heart was still bitter towards

Tiana, he missed her friends. They were great women. "I guess we can get going."

"Sure," she grabbed her purse and notepad, "I have a lot of great homes to show you today."

Throughout the day, Rocio showed Kieran a variety of million-dollar homes. They were all nice but they were missing that one thing, that special something that he needed. He knew what it was—warmth, comfort and love—something he couldn't get from being in a home. No, it had to have been what was in the home. The messy kitchen, the sticky floors, the crayon on the walls, the toys lying around everywhere. The giggles, the coos, the cries. That's what he missed. He missed his family. He missed the family he created and hoped for with Tiana.

"We have one more home to look at," Rocio navigated down the street, "and then we'll be done. It's the last one."

"Okay," Kieran agreed. He didn't want to look at any more homes but he figured one more couldn't hurt.

Rocio pulled up to the last home and turned off the car. "Okay, we're here. This one should be *very* familiar to you."

Kieran looked out the window. He recognized the home, alright. It was Tiana's. "I'm not interested," he quietly replied.

"Oh, I think you are," Rocio got out of the car, "wait until you see the inside!"

Kieran let out a frustrated sigh and silently cursed Rocio. He should've known the moment he saw her back at the office she was up to something. She was extra bubbly and friendly that day. He begrudgingly got out of the car and followed her to the front door. "Whatever it is you two are doing, I want no part of it," he warned.

Rocio looked back at Kieran. "She's smart in business but stupid in love. And you know how people are when they're in love? They do some pretty strange things for the ones they love."

"Like plotting a fake house-showing day?" Kieran smarted back.

"You call it plotting," Rocio rang the doorbell, "I call it creative planning. Have fun." She then walked back to her car and drove off.

Kieran let out another quiet breath. He didn't know what Tiana was planning but he was already annoyed with her. He didn't want her to flaunt her happy relationship in front of his face. He didn't care about what Christopher was up to or how their failed relationship had a second wind. But he stayed for only one reason. He was curious to see how Tyson was holding up. He definitely cared about the little boy.

The door opened a short while later and Kieran felt the air escape his lungs. His ex-girlfriend looked gorgeous as ever. Her natural hair was curly and had grown a little. She had a heartwarming smile on her face. The biggest change was Tyson. He was almost a year old and he seemed to have grown like a weed within the past month. Kieran almost didn't recognize him.

"I'm glad Rocio talked you into staying," Tiana offered as she held Tyson.

"I didn't want to, but she left before I could change my mind," Kieran was honest, "I'm glad to see you're doing well."

"I am," Tiana nodded, "you look good."

"Thank you," Kieran did a glance over at Tiana's frame. She'd put on a little weight around her middle but she still looked amazing. "So do you."

Tiana gave a half-grin. "Can we talk for a moment? It's pretty important."

"Sure," Kieran stepped inside the home and followed Tiana to the living room area. She set Tyson down on the floor and sat with him. Kieran followed her lead. "So what did you want to talk to me about?"

"When Erin got married, that entire week I was feeling crazy. You and I just broke up and things with Christopher weren't any better. I buried myself in my work. Christopher's play of wanting us to be back together and be a family was just that—an act. He didn't last five minutes here."

"So, I don't understand," Kieran resisted the urge to play with Tyson, despite how much he wanted to, "what does that have to do with me?"

"Like I've said, I was feeling crazy. My body temperature was through the roof and my appetite was insane. I would be hungry again even though I just finished eating. At Erin's wedding, I ended up fainting. When I came to at the hospital, that's when I got the diagnosis," Tiana paused before she continued, "I got the diagnosis I was seven-weeks pregnant. I'm ten weeks now."

Kieran was quiet upon the revelation. He quickly did the mental math and thought about the timing; they conceived around the time of the trip back home to Staten Island. His mother knew what she was talking about when she mentioned rainbows.

He wanted to be a father to Tiana's baby but he also respected her wishes. "Whatever you want to do with the baby, I won't fight you," he began, "I know you're busy with your career and with Tyson, so whatever you want to do in terms of the pregnancy, I won't fight you."

"I don't want you to be my baby's daddy, Kieran," Tiana spoke.

Kieran let out a soft sigh and felt his heart crumble. "I understand…"

"I want you to be my husband," Tiana cut him off.

Kieran looked up at her. "What?"

Tiana scooted closer to Kieran and grabbed his hand. "Breaking up with you was by far the dumbest thing I have ever done. I wanted this life for me and Tyson and I foolishly thought I could get it with Christopher when you were by my side all along. You brought out the best in me and you've always encouraged me to just be me and not anyone or anything else.

"You've been more of a father to Tyson and I've seen how he is when he's with you. He loves you! My friends love you and my parents…my hard-ass parents just adore you. I know I'm not the easiest and I still have a lot of growing up to do myself. But if you give me a second chance, if you give *us* a second chance, I promise you won't regret it."

Kieran was silent for a long while before he spoke again. "Normally I don't give second chances, especially to those who hurt me," he said, "but you're a risk I'm willing to take." He kissed her hand and tears streamed down Tiana's cheeks. "So what do we do now?"

"I want you to move back to *our* home," Tiana sniffled. "I want you to put in the paperwork to officially adopt Tyson and finally, I want us to…" She paused.

"You want us to what, *bella*?" Kieran asked.

"I want us to go down to city hall and get married as soon as possible!" Tiana smiled. "I don't think I'm able to fit into any wedding dress right about now."

"Sounds good to me," Kieran smiled. He then placed a hand on her womb. "Forever, I'm yours."

"Forever, I'm yours," Tiana replied back.

Tyson crawled to Kieran and sat in his lap. He reached up and grabbed his face. "Da-da," he cooed.

"That's right," Kieran blinked back tears, "I am your Daddy. And I promise to protect you and Mommy."

****

Kieran stared down at a peacefully sleeping Tyson. It had only been a few weeks but it seemed like ages since he'd seen the little boy. He had gotten so big and started to resemble Tiana in many ways. Kieran was grateful for that. It was bad enough Christopher was Tyson's natural father; the poor child shouldn't look like him as well.

"The way you love and dote on him seems surreal to me at times," Tiana cooed from the doorway.

"Maybe it's because I never had a father who gave a damn," Kieran caressed Tyson's head, "and I didn't want any child of mine to go through the same thing."

Tiana stood beside Kieran and glanced down at their son. "I am so lucky to have you back in my life."

"You're going have to force me out next time," Kieran warned, "because I'm not leaving without a fight."

"I don't want you to," Tiana grabbed Kieran's hand. She pulled him in for a kiss and her body lit up with ecstasy. He moved his lips down her neck and planted small kisses as his hands roamed over her body. Tiana softly moaned as she remembered his touch, his caress, and his love. "What do you want to do now?"

Kieran picked up Tiana and carried her to their bedroom. He quickly undressed as Tiana soon removed her clothing. He rejoined her on the bed and nestled between her legs, his cock teasing her entrance. "I guess we have to practice on you keeping quiet."

"Oh?" Tiana opened her legs wider to accommodate her fiancée. "And how do you suppose we do that?"

Kieran entered Tiana and her body arched in pleasure. He dipped his head down and captured a nipple in his mouth, playing with the dark cherry rosebud. He looked back up and smiled down at his fiancée. Her lips were pursed together and pleasure etched across her face. "I guess we have to see, don't we?" He began to move inside her. "Is this pussy mine? Tell me."

Tiana licked her lips and softly bit them. She couldn't think straight at the moment and Kieran was demanding a solid answer. "Kieran, baby…"

"Tell me," he continued to thrust inside, "is this my pussy? Forever?"

"It's all yours, baby," Tiana pulled Kieran in for a kiss, "it's yours forever."

The couple held hands as they moved in unison, solidifying their union once again as they climbed higher and higher to new orgasmic heights. Throughout the night they would continue the dance until they were too exhausted to continue.

EPILOGUE

Four years later…

"Remember, you need to have at least eight months of emergency savings in today's economy. Don't worry about how long it'll take you to save, trust me. Once you get into the habit of saving and investing your money, you'll be hard-pressed to spend it on frivolous stuff. If you have to put it on credit, that means you can't afford it. It's better to have money in the bank, than wearing your money to impress people you don't like or care about. That concludes tonight's program on the Tiana Morris show," she smiled to the camera, "as always, stay beautiful and blessed, family. See you next week."

"And we're clear!" The director yelled. "Great show as always, Tiana! How are you feeling up there?"

Allison rushed to Tiana's side to help her out of the chair. "I feel like I'm about to explode any minute now," she rubbed her growing tummy.

"Well, you are due any day," Allison commented, "I'm surprised Kieran still let you work."

"I didn't have a choice. He *forced* me out of the home," Tiana sighed, "I was getting on his nerves."

"You? Getting on Kieran's nerves? Get out of here!" Allison laughed.

"Yeah, yeah, real cute. Remember who's still paying you every month," Tiana smiled.

"So, are you finally going to go on maternity leave?" Allison asked. "We're still taking bets on if you're going to have the baby here."

"Yes, this was the last show for a while. I'll be out for several weeks and back in here in no time," Tiana waddled to her dressing room.

She opened up the dressing room door to see her family behind it. "What did you think of tonight's show?"

Kieran bounced their four-year-old daughter, Gianna, on his lap while Tyson got up from the floor and gave his mom a big hug. Their other son, two-year-old Angelo, was sleeping on a nearby sofa. "I thought it was great," Kieran glanced over to look at his notes, "and your contractions seem to be steady as well."

After a whirlwind wedding at the courthouse, Kieran moved back in with Tiana the same day. Christopher relinquished his parental rights, paving the way for Kieran to adopt Tyson. Kieran's child care business expanded to a clothing line, Tyson's Heart, with Tyson being front and center. The clothing was affordably priced for everyone, no matter what income level. The clothing line had seen its profits triple over the past year due to word of mouth and sales.

Tiana sold her investment firm and signed a lucrative offer from a major network to host a weekly hour-long program giving out financial advice and tips. She was currently booked well into the next year for a book tour and seminars. Professionally, she went by her maiden name but in all of her social circles, she was Tiana D'Amato.

"The ear-pulling method seems to be the most incognito of everything else we've tried." Tiana breathed, "Not quite rushing to the hospital worthy, but I'm thinking this baby will be here before my birthday on Wednesday."

Kieran got up and gave his wife a kiss. "It'll be a lovely birthday gift. My mom's flight should be coming in tomorrow afternoon and she'll stay for a couple weeks while Eli and Joey run the shops in her absence."

"That's great. She can stay longer if she wants to, like forever," Tiana smiled.

"We have a nanny, Tiana," Kieran reminded her, "and we're paying *him* very well."

"I don't know why you were so insistent he had to have been gay," she blinked her eyes.

"It was the only reasonable solution that worked for both of us," Kieran picked up Angelo and grabbed Gianna's hand, "besides I know how you are with the help."

"And how am I with the help?" She smiled.

Kieran motioned to their children and Tiana's womb. "Really?"

Tiana smiled sheepishly. "You know this is the last one, right?"

"I promise," he kissed her forehead.

Tyson tugged on his mother's dress and Tiana bent down to talk to him. "Well, you know the rules. Ask your father," she nudged him, "go on."

"Dad, can I have that Tonka truck for my birthday?" Tyson asked with big puppy eyes. "Please? Pretty please?"

"I recognize that look," Kieran raised an eyebrow, "it's the same look your mother gives me when she wants a foot rub."

"Well, he's learned from the best," Tiana smiled.

"Sure thing, Ty. I'll get it for you," Kieran smiled at Tiana, "and is there anything Mommy wants?"

"Of course," Tiana smiled, "a foot rub!"

THE END

207

OTHER TITLES BY VERA ROBERTS:

DEAR DIARY

DISCIPLINE (SCOTT & MARIANA)

GETTIN' IT

HOT LIKE FIRE (SWEET AND CLEAN ROMANCE)

S&M III, VOL. II (SCOTT & MARIANA)

S&M III, VOL. I (SCOTT & MARIANA)

S&M II (SCOTT & MARIANA)

S&M (SCOTT & MARIANA)

THE TRAIN RIDE (FREE ON SMASHWORDS.COM)

THE EROTIC INTOXICATION, VOL. I: BAD GIRLS

THE PAINTER

TIL TOMORROW

FACEBOOK PAGE:

WWW.FACEBOOK.COM/MS.VERA.ROBERTS

BLOG:

WWW.VERAROBERTS.COM

Made in the USA
San Bernardino, CA
12 March 2013